# MIAMI VICE
## 1: THE FLORIDA BURN

As Crockett bent to pick up the sunglasses he spotted something under the Chevy. A flat black package, like a birthday present, taped to the sloping curve of the enormous mid-sixties gas tank.

His brain stalled for just one second while all the facts rushed together and made a picture.

Still jiving, Corky shoved the key into the car's lock and twisted.

'No – !' Crockett yelled, trying vainly to reach twenty yards and jerk Eddie back.

The tail end of the Chevy blew apart in a billowing orange fireball that consumed Eddie, Corky, and a hundred thousand dollars' worth of cocaine.

# MIAMI VICE
# 1: THE FLORIDA RUN

A novel by
## Stephen Grave

Based on the Universal television series '*Miami Vice*'
Created by Anthony Yerkovich
Adapted from the pilot episode '*Miami Vice*'
Written by Anthony Yerkovich

A STAR BOOK
*published by*
the Paperback Division of
W.H. Allen & Co. PLC

A Star Book
Published in 1985
by the Paperback Division of
W.H. Allen & Co. PLC
44 Hill Street, London W1X 8LB

Copyright © 1985 by MCA Publishing, a Division of
MCA, Inc. All rights reserved.

Printed and bound in Great Britain by
Anchor Brendon Ltd, Tiptree, Essex

ISBN 0 352 316942

For
# TOM STRUCK
*who sends me stuff*
*and has more interesting vices than I can count*

*vice:* moral depravity or corruption; habitual, abnormal behaviour patterns detrimental to health or usefulness; sexual immorality, esp. prostitution.

*vice squad:* police squad charged with enforcement of laws concerning gambling, pornography, prostitution and the illegal use of liquor and narcotics.

# 1

*The deal is going down,* thought Tubbs, and about the deal he couldn't care less.

Everything reminded him of his brother, and how his brother had bought it. What was the joke? *Try not to think of a pink elephant.* He tried, tried hard not to think of how Raphael had died. He tried to imagine Raphael was not dead. It was stupid; it never worked. Raphael had told him the one about the pink elephant when Tubbs was fifteen. It was one of those little, jokey things that somehow stuck with you all your life – he'd never forget it. And pretending would not erase the fact that Raphael was gone.

The wind outside was icecube cold and there was a foot of black slush crowded up against the curbs. The street was wet, oily, and black; the deep stress furrows in the tarmac formed a peculiar relief pattern that stretched away from Tubbs to merge at some infinity point beyond the reach of his vision. Tubbs hated Queens. The Bogota North section of Jackson Heights was like a bombed-out DMZ – fire-charred, boarded-up storefronts, dead animals frozen under the snow, crumbling brownstone tenements, streetlamps blown out in anger, the occasional hulk of a wrecked and stripped automobile consumed by fire. It looked as though cars simply blew themselves to smithereens if they had been parked in this neighbourhood too long, committing suicide rather than staying in this part of town.

The car Tubbs waited in was – had been – Raphael's, a diamond-black Chrysler brougham with buff leather upholstery. The harsh winter had sandblasted away some of the showroom shine. Inside, the car smelled as new as it had when Raphael had first tooled it home. Tubbs had killed the running lights and dashboard telltales; he sat alone in the darkness, a silhouette on the dead and ominous street.

He glanced down at his digital Seiko. God, was it really three o'clock in the a.m.? He huffed out a sigh and rubbed the blur from his eyes.

Two buildings down, a pair of ragged Puerto Rican hopheads tried vainly to warm their grimy and threadbare mitts over a smelly trashcan fire. *San Juan Clambake*, thought Tubbs, watching the firelight dance in the beads of water that speckled the windshield and hood of the Chrysler. He pulled his own gloved hands from his armpits and groped around for his thermos jug of coffee. He'd brewed up some Amaretto grind; its rich, pungent smell eddied around inside the Chrysler's cabin. There was a slug of Kahlua floating around in the bottom of the jug. Tubbs agitated it and poured out half a cup. It was only lukewarm now.

The burnouts stoking the trashcan fire jabbered at each other – fast jive, contoured by crystal meth, or maybe just a snort or two of carburettor cleaner. God only knew what was wrapped in the brown bag they swigged from. Cheap port mixed with aftershave? Sterno cocktail? A shot of wood alcohol with an airplane glue chaser?

He drained the plastic cup and refocused his eyes on a surgical steel grey AMG Mercedes, parked a block and a half down on the opposite side of the street, a Latino car

8

stripper's dream. Tubbs knew he was not visible to the driver of the other car; he'd worked tails with Raphael before and knew how to stay out of sight. After twenty-five yards the chrome on the Chrysler just looked like more snow, and the junkie fire was between them. Plumes of exhaust periodically chuffed from the Mercedes and spun up into the chilly air. The driver was working his heater.

Tubbs thumped his feet against the firewall carpeting. His ass was starting to buzz with numbness. He fancied he heard music.

Wait a second – he *did* hear music. His ears identified the bridge from 'Miss You', by the Stones. Jagger was pushing it out about sleeping all alone, now *that* was a giggle.

It was behind him. He caught movement in the rearview. Two – no, three dudes, prowling along in the dark. Fatigue jackets, Army surplus boots for stomping, battered porkpie toppers. The mirror threw back the glint of a suitcase-sized ghetto blaster that pumped out the tunes. Tubbs did not turn around.

The music got louder, and moved around to the driver's side window. After a second a sawed-off glove tapped knuckles on Tubbs' glass hard enough to make little pellets of water roll downward.

'Say! Bro!'

*Louder, scumwad,* Tubbs thought, and the Mercedes would notice. The dudes wanted trouble. They owned the street. He'd have to deal with them.

A fist, now, banging the safety glass. 'Yo! My man!'

Tubbs cranked down the window and stared at them with the expression of a man who has just found a dead fly in his chicken sandwich.

The foremost punk cracked a serpent's grin and planted his hands on the doorjamb. All three were

9

Latinos. The one with the stereo stood furthest back, legs aggressively apart. Dumb punk had been watching too many rock videos, thought Tubbs. The second one had his hands in his pockets – he'd be the one to watch, while the first one would do the talking. Tubbs knew the drill. As his left hand had rolled down the window, his right had cleared away his thermos and gone beneath a knit blanket covering the other half of the front seat.

'Got a couple of twenties I can hold, brother?'

'I'm not your damned brother,' Tubbs said, flat and low.

'Say what?' The first punk nodded and his confederate hocked and blew a cloudy spitwad onto the front windshield. It oozed downward. 'Like I say, we need the twenties to hold for the wash 'n' wax, man.'

Nothing had happened with the Mercedes... but Tubbs couldn't afford to screw around with these dudes. He looked up at the leader. 'Beat it.'

The trio cracked up in the overblown laughter of the terminally macho adolescent. ''Dis chuck think's he's Michael Jackson or something!' Yuck-yuck-yuck. Then the confederate made his move, flashing out an Army bayonet from the depths of his coat. The blade was dull black, at least ten inches long.

Tubbs saw it coming, and tilted up the chopped-off barrels of the 12-gauge shotgun he had slid across his lap. When he pulled back both hammers they made a sound like breaking teeth, and the complexion of the dude with the knife suddenly went a very cheesy colour despite the cold. The twin bores were six inches away from Motormouth's solar plexus.

'Can it wait, bro?' said Tubbs. 'I'm kinda busy right now.'

The dude had both hands up and open to show he wasn't packed. The knife vanished. Everybody backed away with frozen, corpselike grins. 'Oh, absolutely...'

The Stones tape ran out with a squawk.

'Nice rappin' with ya, my man...'

They were gone, blending back into the night, making careful tracks back the way they'd come. Not *too* quickly – there were egos to be preserved.

He wondered vaguely if the guy in the Mercedes had made him. Apparently not. He allowed himself a brief flash of paranoia that suggested the junkies near the fire might be watchdogs for Calderone. One of them swooned on his feet and plopped backwards into an alley slush-bank, staying down. His comrade moved over to him, removed the bottle in its brown bag, and returned to the fire.

These guys were no lookouts. Calderone would have them on the street corners. They'd be more like the trio of Latino punks, only serious.

The dark building disgorged a little group of people. Expensive overcoats. Medium-sized Haliburton suitcase toted by a highly paid South American killer. Another equally ugly gorilla in expensive clothes just for show. And in the middle, Francisco Calderone. Curly, silver-black hair swept backwards from a front-end peak flanked by two bald spots. His eyes were black-coffee dark and dead of expression, the highlights in them like Mexican silver, artificial somehow. Like many short men, Calderone had compensated by trying to become big in other ways. The suitcase was loaded with cash or dope or both. Calderone was big in the dope trade, Raphael had once told Tubbs.

That had been the understatement of the century. Calderone, the mean little man with the pocky face, *was* the dope trade for much of the East Coast, including New York, which was crammed to the spires with folks eager to shell out large amounts of money in exchange for white powder to shove up their noses, or plug into major veins. Stupid way to be hip, thought Tubbs.

The killer without the suitcase played chauffeur and helped Calderone into the right rear of the Mercedes with one hand. His other hand was stuffed in his overcoat pocket, probably wrapped around a Magnum; or more likely it was stuck through a hole in the coat lining and held the stock of an Uzi submachine gun.

That brought the memory back, full blast.

*The deal was going down. Raphael and his partner, a white dude named Jake Bartamas, were playing the buyers, setting up Calderone for an A-1 bust on the Brooklyn waterfront. Raphael was wearing Gianni Versace threads and looking high class, all dealer-cool. A couple of Columbians; another Haliburton. Raphael flashed the cash, a calf-hide briefcase full of banded stacks of fifties, fifty bills to a stack. Raphael had been dogging Calderone for months, undercover. Tubbs watched from twenty-five yards away. He and two backup men were hidden behind a crated shipment of Milanese hemp. He could see Calderone sitting in the rear seat of an airport limousine. His window was down; he oversaw the deal. Tubbs saw him nod significantly. The Columbians opened up the Haliburton. When Raphael and Jake saw the stash, they'd arrest everybody, and Tubbs, his men, and another group of backups near the waterfront warehouse would move in and sweep up. The case opened. The Columbians pulled out cocked Uzis. Tubbs screamed a warning but it was drowned out in the blatting stammer of automatic weapons fire. Raphael's chest came apart, spoiling his new suit. Pieces of Jake Bartamas flew into the Atlantic Ocean. Raphael collapsed in a spray of his own blood and didn't twitch. Tubbs was up and running. The Columbians jumped into the limo as return fire banged uselessly against the car's armour plating. It sped away into the night.*

*Tubbs leapt over Jake's unmoving corpse. He held his brother's head. His hands immediately became wet and sticky. Raphael's eyes connected with his. 'Looks like I blew it,' they said, unapologetic. Raphael tried to clasp Tubbs' hand but his body would no longer obey the orders of his brain. The hand jerked like a speared fish and was still. Raphael's eyes glazed over, he exhaled, and he was as dead as a pipedream. Tubbs stayed there, cradling his brother's head until the useless ambulances screeched up.*

Calderone had nodded his head, and Raphael had become history. That was life.

The Mercedes tried a U-turn, came up short thanks to the ice clogging the street, backed up, cleared it. Tubbs watched the tail-lights a second before turning over his own engine.

As he pulled away from the curb, forty pounds worth of loaded trashcan hit the vacated space like a ghetto ICBM. It split a seam on impact and scattered garbage into the street. Tubbs glanced back, and saw the Latino punks giving him a one-finger salute from the top of the building.

*Y tu, vatos*, he thought, and drove away.

Calderone's vehicle took Atlantic Avenue and headed for the Brooklyn Bridge. Tubbs followed it across, keeping two blocks back as they came into the Bronx.

More slummed-out real estate. It seemed to go on forever, dank and grey, wet and unrelenting, the sleep-grogged, drugged-out, ticked-off bad side of the tough, New York profile. Tubbs himself was a Big Apple boy, and maintained a provincial love for this overblown, noisy human waste dump and three-ring circus... it was required of any native son. The town might lack restraint, but it had everything, and beat life in the Wheat Belt hands-down. Problem was, such a cosmopolitan outlook allowed scumbones like Calderone to thrive, parasites on the social organism.

For his dining and drinking pleasure in the pre-dawn, Calderone had chosen an establishment called Huge Tommy's, right in the heart of the war zone. It was a monolithic nineteenth-century warehouse that had been converted into an after-hours club, and Tubbs knew the front door was actually bomb-proof. A parking valet jumped from foot to foot under the blue floodlight near the front canopy, freezing his ass off. Calderone's limo went into a holding pattern behind an obscene looking pink-pearl-and-chrome Corsair stretch job, three hundred grand on wheels, complete with hot tub. It pulled to the door and vomited out a Keystone Kops gaggle of monied Iranians with two grand's worth of Gucci covering their feet and a wardrobe that violated a good taste ordinance or two. The Son of the Sheik, thought Tubbs, times five. Poor little rich boys on the slum-thrills ride. Their limo tooled away and Calderone's nosed into the debarkation zone. Calderone stepped out, as lithe as a Cuban dancer, and entered the club between his two goons.

Tubbs killed his engine and stashed his sawed-off shotgun beneath the front seat, stuffing the blanket in behind it. From the glove compartment he broke out a police-issue .357 Magnum loaded with wadcutters and jammed it into the break-away upside-down shoulder holster rig he was already wearing.

He strolled nonchalantly to the blast door and nodded at the doorman, who rolled his eyes and looked elsewhere. The door swung inward and a shock-blast of high-powered synthesizer music rattled his guts. Inside it was as glittery as a Korean jewelry shop, all flash and filigree and high-decibel, mind-creaming, skull-pulsing sound. Incredibly, Tubbs recognized it as a disco

14

permutation of Rod Stewart's 'Do Ya Think I'm Sexy?'.

He wandered into the wall-to-wall crowd and mingled, tacking on the bar, which ran the entire length of the east wall and caged-in at least four full time 'tenders. The colours were the glitzy neon of a Quaalude nightmare, strobing and flashing, sequined and spangled. The odours were of over-priced perfume and the earthy sweat of the mating dance. It was too much for the eyes to swallow in one gulp, certainly a slap-in-the-face contrast to the Real World outside.

The bar seemed to be made out of a mile-long hunk of solid Italian quarry marble, and expensive crystal fixtures. Around him, both skin and century notes were flashed with calculated abandon. Smarmy designer jean magnates slapped down exhausted moves, trying to pick up a bored-looking chicken before the sun rose. Coked-out ingénues assessed the fish surrounding them and selected their kills. Nouvelle hip bag men clinked glasses with four-bill-per-night hookers. Pieces of jailbait in black leather smoked Gauloises and squinted, looking for kicks. Lacking kicks, they'd take anything negotiable. Upscale pot smugglers flaunted their lack of style by swigging Budweiser from the bottle. Tubbs looked over his shoulder and said, 'Martel,' to the nearest barkeep. A snifter clinked on the marble in response, and Tubbs took a whiff before sipping.

The glass to his face, he spotted Calderone's table just as a waiter wheeled away from it. Tubbs followed the white coat through the throng with his eyes until it parked at the bar and loaded up a tray with a magnum of Cristal – authentic French pretentiousness for fifty bucks a bottle – six flutes and some mixed drinks full of ice. Tubbs caught the guy's attention as he passed on his way back.

Tubbs leaned close, and his whisper was understood even against the din of the crowd and the thumping music. The waiter nodded and pocketed the hundred-dollar bill Tubbs had pressed into his palm.

A woman with mountain-pass cleavage and pink and blonde hair was shouting into his ear.

'What?' Tubbs yelled back.

She held up a tiny silver straw in invitation. 'Gotta go powder my nose,' she said, eyes twinkling with an all-night high. 'There's room for two in my backseat. Wanna come?'

The waiter did his act. After setting the Cristal and fluted glasses on Calderone's table, he overcorrected and sent the mixed drinks into the lap of the drug kingpin. Total calamity. Calderone bolted to his feet in a torrent of Spanish epithets directed at the waiter, who bowed and scraped and looked up from the floor long enough to get his face slapped. The little Columbian was livid with anger at this horrendous social *gaffe*. It had happened in front of guests – in this case, two middle-aged entrepreneurs of questionable means and a trio of jaded, drug-dazed aerobics lovelies turned out in silk sheaths and spikes. They looked like the world's most desperate Eileen Ford protégées. When the waiter grabbed up a wad of cocktail napkins and tried to blot Calderone's silk suit, the bodyguards, who were posted several yards off to either side of the choice booth, rushed to protect their master with Doberman speed and ferocity. Tubbs grinned to himself. It was worth the century note just to watch the frenetic display. The goons pulled the waiter and shoved him away. He brushed his lapels, shot his cuffs, and glided back to the bar, his extra tip fully earned. One of the party girls hid a laugh behind a napkin. More babbling; everyone was offering to help Calderone, as Tubbs had hoped. He brushed them off with an exaggerated gesture. *No, no, really, I'm all right, it's okay, I just gotta go to the men's room, you know?* He backed out of the group. The bodyguards restored order at the booth. The paunchy nobodies sat down and resumed groping the party girls. Calderone weaved through the crowd and made for the neon-lit corridor marked RESTROOMS – TELE-PHONES – FIRE EXIT in two languages.

'Am I crazy or are you not paying any attention to me?' said the pink-blonde with the over-eager chest. She blinked mock-innocently and cracked her gum.

'You're beautiful, honey,' Tubbs assured her, 'but I gotta go see a man about a giraffe.' He patted her cheek and moved into the throng.

Calderone's bodyguards had not followed him to the john.

Tubbs ducked quickly into the corridor. Checking his piece for loads was stupid; he knew it was loaded, and he knew what those loads could do. Wadcutters pancaked when they hit, and tore away a lot of gristle, sloppily.

Twelve paces to the men's room door. Tubbs stalled while two spacey bits of fluff reeled out of the women's room and staggered, arm-in-arm, in his direction.

'Ooh, a little chocolate bunny,' said the one with the bleached-out punk 'do. 'C'mon with us, darling, you're *cute*!'

'What about Ramon?' said her partner, whose eyes were invisible behind crusting layers of Cleopatra makeup.

'To hell with Ramon,' said the first, gobbling Tubbs up with her eyes.

From behind Tubbs a voice said, 'Both of you flake away, right now.' He was too close to Tubbs to be an errant pedestrian.

Tubbs speed-drew his pistol and dodged low while a

17

heavy haymaker blow sliced the air where his head had been. He brought the .357 up and down with a knifelike action, and smashed the interloper's nose into cartilaginous pulp. Blood spurted floorward from both nostrils, making a letter A on his face, with the mouth as the crossbar. His eyes had one second to register surprise before they rolled up into dreamland. It was one of Calderone's goons, as Tubbs had anticipated.

What he hadn't anticipated was the second one, crashing through the doorway and charging him like a fullback. The two punk flappers screamed. He ploughed into Tubbs headfirst. Tubbs landed on his can and skidded backwards, the air woofing out of him. He had dropped his pistol. The goon was still clawing his own gun out. More screams.

Tubbs levered up from the floor and kicked the bodyguard hard in the wrist, whipping him around and sending the gun cartwheeling away. A freight-train fist aimed for his face and he bobbed around it. The goon lumbered past. Tubbs planted two sharp jabs into his kidneys. The goon grunted nasally and turned for another charge.

Calderone was looking at the fight from the men's room door. Tubbs realized that time was up.

He flathanded the goon in the face, jumped and locked his forearms around his head, bent him over and kicked the wind out of him until he coughed blood. Growing up on the streets of New York had taught Tubbs all sorts of cute combat tricks. He dropped the goon atop the inert form of his partner. Calderone had already disappeared out the fire exit. The door hissed shut on its hydraulic closure and Tubbs smashed into the bar before it was fully shut.

The door flew back and banged metallically against the outside wall. No sign of Calderone.

He'd forgotten his gun. *Damn it!* He spun widdershins. No sign of life at all. Calderone had blended into the scenery with the speed of a cockroach. Stupid, foolhardy to chase a man who was probably packed, thought Tubbs, when he'd lost his own gun.

He did it anyway. He ran down the alley, leather shoes kicking up puddles of slush. At a noise to his left, he froze, fully expecting a bullet in the spleen.

A scrawny, rib-protruding Bronx alley dog ravaged the spillings from an overturned garbage can. It glanced up at Tubbs, snarled, and returned to his late dinner.

Tubbs' shoulders drooped. His ragged breath made wispy contrails in the chill air. His stomach throbbed from the dent Calderone's hound dog had put in his midsection.

Calderone was nowhere to be seen. He had escaped again, like a wraith.

## 2

*The deal is going down*, thought Crockett, *as it damned well better*! Stringing a 1960s acid casualty like Corky Fowler along, even for four days, was a trial. Crockett was used to undercover vice work, and had lived weeks, *months*, playing roles – cocaine buyer, smuggler, biker assassin-for-hire, pornographer – and assumed his roles with an intensity unparalleled on the squad. His cover was perfect and his record was star-studded, just as his personal life was a blown-out minefield of disasters. He wore a Basile linen suit (top o' the line confiscated goods, guaranteed to up his status as homegrown pusher/smuggler/smut monger) over a green Atlanta University jersey, numbered 88 and damp at the pits. Something about Corky Fowler gnawed at him; he didn't *want* to trust the guy, but he'd been four days setting up a fair sized buy that might lead him to the Columbian... and *that* brass ring Crockett had been chasing for what they call 'a powerful long time, ma'am,' on the bad Westerns he frequently found himself staring at alone about two in the morning.

The Columbian. Crockett's personal Professor Moriarty these past few months. Even Eddie Rivera cocked his head a funny way when Crockett started going on about *The Columbian*. Jeez, they probably thought he was ready for medical R & R, he mused. But today, thanks to the Corky connection, Crockett might be able to stash the Columbian in a bag and deliver the sleazeball with a bright red ribbon wrapped around his head. He chuckled to himself. Lieutenant Rodriguez would faint dead away.

Crockett was jolted back to reality by a blast from the rubber-spined black kid breaking and popping on the corner nearest the Coconut Grove Café. Something awful was gushing out of the boom-box woofers on the kid's radio, a gleaming slum PA system at least as big as Crockett's desk back at Division headquarters. It sounded like distorted Prince. The kid was a wonder to behold, but Crockett was annoyed. Only in America, he thought, could something as moronic as break-dancing catch on in a big way.

Rivera sauntered out of the café, noshing on a hunk of Danish. 'You sure you don't want some Excedrin or something?' he said airily. 'Y'know, for your ... ah, head problem?' Big joke.

'Five thousand street corners in greater Miami, and Gumby there has gotta pick *ours*.' He winced when the sun-flash from the three pounds of gold jewelry Rivera was wearing slugged him in the retinas. Beautiful Florida sunshine, like orange juice for the brain.

Crockett hated orange juice.

He inhaled deeply, rubbed his aching eyes, and dropped his dark-tinted Vuarnetas back over them. 'So anyhow,' he said, picking up the conversation Eddie had interrupted to grab a bite, 'you got mad. Lost 'ya temper, am I right? Worked your jowls and did the hot-blooded Latin machismo number and stomped out of the house, hm?' He deliberately pronounced it mah-*chiz*-mo, to tick Eddie off.

His partner didn't rise to the bait. 'Something like that. It embarrasses me now. Like it was a scene out of a bad soap opera, you know – all those lines you never

21

thought you'd hear coming out of your own face.'

'Y'mean like, "I don't want the mother of my children working in some greasy spoon"?'

Eddie sighed. 'She's due in five months, man.'

'Maria *knows* how tough it is raising a family on the kind of bread we make, my man.' He snorted. 'Hell, a baby buggy alone'll put you back a week's take-home.'

Eddie folded his arms. 'No wife of mine oughta have to work for a living...'

'Another line, Eddie.'

'Yeah. Dumb, huh?' He shifted uncomfortably under all his necklaces; he wasn't used to playing Mr Filthy Rich West Coast Buyer. Eddie went more for the combat end of Vice. 'I feel like that buff black dude on the TV; you know, the one with the mohawk and all the gold?'

Crockett wasn't listening. He was staring with distaste back toward the juvenile breaker. 'Hey, shortstop, y'wanna crank down the decibels a notch?'

One of the kid's compadres shot a poisonous look back, leaned over and turned the ghetto-blaster up a good ten percent. Bystanders, mostly trendies from the Grove, staggered backwards, their tossed change missing the kid's upended porkpie hat. Crockett winced.

When he turned back, Eddie had the pocket tin of Excedrin in his hand. Crockett turned three of the tablets out into his palm and took them dry, crunching them up before swallowing. 'The cure,' he said. 'Swear by it.'

'So where the hell's Corky?'

'He'll show. I was up till four a.m. trading shots of Cuervo Gold with the little bozo just to close the deal. He'll show or I'll have Elvis devour him.'

'First Corky, then the Columbian, huh?'

'You win a cookie.'

'How 'bout a dime instead?'

Crockett saw the light. 'You going to call Maria?'

'Yeah.' Eddie gave a sheepish little shrug. 'I want to tell her how much I appreciate how she's busting a gut to help out. Maybe take her out to dinner tonight at Antonio's. Dance a little. Make up for this morning.'

Crockett dug for loose change. 'Now you're talking, ace.' If he had done as much for Caroline, had been as considerate, maybe she wouldn't be filing for divorce now, he thought ruefully.

Eddie had turned to make for the pay phone when Crockett spotted Corky's totally awesome, entirely tasteless arson-yellow 450 SL convertible. He grabbed Eddie's arm. 'Showtime, son. You'll have to call her later.'

Corky's tyres kicked up grey smoke and screech as he scattered some of the break-dancing kid's audience. The Van Halen on his car deck drowned out the beat of Prince. He was wearing mirrored pilot glasses and had eyes only for Crockett as he pulled to the curb. 'What it *is*, dude!'

'Keep the dime,' Crockett said from the side of his mouth. 'Let me introduce you to Mr Fabulous.'

Eddie matched pace as they walked towards the 450 SL. 'Where'd I just fly in from this time . . . ?'

Crockett had to think a second before he remembered.

'Malibu!' shouted Corky as the freeway slipstream tore through the car and mixed with the traffic noise and heavy metal pounding Crockett's brain-pan. 'That's just too *much*, Eddie! I mean, like, the whole geo-cultural *concept* of it all!'

Crockett was hunched in the back. Eddie rode shotgun, his body providing a partial shield from the over-cranked stereo. Crockett's head was really pounding now. Corky was one of those overcooked surfers who barely missed visiting Vietnam but decided to tax his metabolism with a double truckload of LSD anyway. Most every dendrite of Corky's intelligence had been flash-fried away years ago, leaving a loudmouthed shell whose sole reasons for living included aloha shirts, Valley-Girl-speak, and Def Leppard.

'What?' Eddie yelled back at him.

'I mean, dig it – some dirt-poor beaner way up in the Andes, pickin' his teeth with peyote or something, he tears off a half-ton of cocoa leaves, mule-trains 'em down to Lima, Lima to Bogotá, Bogotá to Miami, Miami to yours truly, me to Eddie, and Eddie to Tinseltown, Lotus Land, Circus Maximus to the *stars*! I *mean*! The business we're in is so . . . worldly, y'know?'

Eddie glanced back at Crockett. The monologue had dazed them both. Corky kept taking his hands off the wheel to wave them around.

Crockett's eyes caught a street sign. He leaned between the seats to be heard 'Hey, spud,' he shouted at Eddie. 'You forget where the ocean is? My boat's in the Atlantic.'

The radio hit a ditch between songs, and what Corky said next came through loud and clear. 'Ain't gonna need your speedboat, dude. Got a different stash, and it's already in.'

Crockett and Eddie were professionals, and did not let this news show on their faces. Crockett's rule was to get hot if any changes came down; that always put the mark on the defensive. 'That ain't the plan, Corky! Eddie here flashes the cash, then we take the boat out and pick up the Columbian's stash –'

Corky wrinkled his lips '*What* Columbian, man, he's old news! I got a whole new supplier.' To Eddie he shot a conspiratorial grin. 'New and improved factory wholesaler, direct to *you* the customer, dude!'

'That's *not* what we agreed on!' Crockett's fire was fanned now that Corky had cut the Columbian out of the deal.

To Corky it was all no sweat. 'Free *enterprise*, dude, the basis of Western Democracy, the thing that made America free! What difference? You sound like you don't wanna make the deal!'

Crockett didn't miss a beat. 'Okay, cowboy, you want to rewrite the game plan, I'll rewrite the rules! It's now thirty-two grand a key, not forty. Half the bread right now, the other half contingent on a purity test back at my boat. And *you're* picking up Eddie's business expenses – hotel bills and airfare from LA, you got it?'

Corky's complexion paled, even in the sun and wind. 'Hey – *hey*, man, I got profit margins to consider, Burnett, and that's a freakin' ripoff, and you know it!'

'Free *enterprise*, dude,' Crockett shot back with a marvellously timed shrug. 'Burnett' was his cover name.

Corky steamed in silence for a mile or two, then gave up. Crockett suspected the only thing that worried Corky for any length of time was where to find the next party. The deal would still go down . . . but without the Columbian. He began to feel like he'd just wasted four days on Corky; a low-rent bust hadn't been what he'd had in mind for this afternoon. But now he and Eddie had to play it out.

Corky signalled that his momentary pique was concluded by jumping back into his rapid-fire, stream-of-consciousness nattering. 'Sometimes I feel guilty, man – y'know, like, all that *money* we make. Y'should send some money back there, man, like, I mean, to Bogotá or Columbia. Y'should send some money there to sponsor a child, or a farmer. Y'know – a nickle a day buys this child enough milk for a week? I always wondered how come they couldn't do that in *this* country – man, I wish I could get a deal like that in my local supermarket, y'know what I mean? But *I* sponsored *two* kids down there, man. Emilio and Maria. They send me letters, pictures of 'em, everything. They're almost like real children.'

There was a moment of oddly appropriate silence, then Corky punched a button on the radio and the 450 SL filled up with raucous electric guitar, abused by someone with a lot of flash and no skill.

'All *riiiight*!' Corky bellowed, turning it up full blast. 'Quiet *riot*!'

Crockett and Eddie sank down in their seats.

Corky's pickup point turned out to be a parked 1965 Chevy Impala stashed under an overpass near Little Havana. There was a cluster of warehouse-type buildings, mostly deserted. They bumped over some railroad tracks on their way to the car. It was a dirty yellow convertible with a black roof featuring deep vertical slashes in the material. Somebody had sanded the car's door-panel rust spots and sealed them, using black spray primer, so the car looked like it had flown through a heavy flak barrage.

There was no one around. They climbed from the 450 SL, Corky and Eddie using the doors, Crockett vaulting over the rear panel. The tendon in his shoulder jumped. He resisted the urge to massage it. Got to watch those old gridiron injuries, he thought.

Corky was off and blabbering again, to Eddie the Malibu Dealer! 'Ninety-two percent, lab-tested, *pure* Peruvian flake, Edward my man. Root canal quality, you hear what I'm sayin'? None of that jumped-on, baby-laxed rat poo they push on the Coast...'

Crockett felt a pain in his rear end. Scooping up Corky, by himself, would be child's play.

Eddie turned, delivering the first line of their divide-and-conquer tactic. 'Say, Burnett – I left my scale behind the seat. You mind?'

'Nope.' He turned back to the Mercedes while Corky fumbled with his keyring, thumbing up those needed to open the Chevy. This gave him an opportunity to pause by the trunk and show off his new watch to Eddie, build a little camaraderie with the customers, that sort of thing. He twisted his wrist and waved the solid gold Rolex under Eddie's nose.

'Twelve *grand*, Edward, cash. I was gonna spring eighteen for the "Presidential", but it just *screams* "dealer", if you know what I mean.'

Eddie nodded and grunted, eyeing the trunk of the Chevy. ''S'nice.'

Crockett – Burnett – retrieved the pharmaceutical scale from the backseat of the Mercedes, and in leaning over his sunglasses slithered from his coat pocket and clattered on the cement.

'Crap,' he muttered. 'Probably scratched the lenses.' As he bent to pick the Vuarnets up, he spotted something under the Chevy. He had to squint through his shades to make it out. A flat black package, like a birthday present, taped to the sloping curve of the typically enormous mid-sixties gas tank.

His brain stalled for just one second while all the facts rushed together and made a picture.

Still jiving, Corky shoved the key into the trunk slot and twisted.

'*No* – !' Crockett yelled, trying vainly to reach twenty yards and jerk Eddie back.

The tail end of the Chevy blew apart in a billowing

orange fireball that consumed Eddie, Corky, and a hundred thousand dollars' worth of cocaine. The heat blast knocked Crockett off his pins; when he opened his eyes he saw the trunk lid of the Chevy flipping end-over-end thirty feet in the air. It was burning. One of the Chevy's tyres rolled past the 450 SL, smoking. It looked like the vehicle had been hit by a jolt of Army-issue napalm and flattened. Neither the dope dealer nor Crockett's partner were in any way visible or evident. They had been erased by the explosion. Flames rolled into the sky.

Crockett sat there, legs stupidly splayed, head reeling, the scale still in one hand.

What was left of the Chevy plumed thick black smoke upward. It would guide the police so they could be too late.

Switek and Zito arrived at the scene before even the ambulances – for all the good they'd do – showed up.

Ernest Switek and Tommy Ray Zito were the plainclothes vice team's hamburger-and-hotdog combo. Switek was bearish and *lumpen*, like a biker keeping a muscular rein on a beer gut, and hiding whatever smarts he possessed behind a dense brush of reddish-brown beard. Zito, by physical contrast, was a gaunt ectomorph, blade-thin and glassy-eyed, all bones and overtight guitar-string sinews. He usually had a tooth-pick or a cigarette hanging out of his face, and his finger-nails were gnawed down to the quick, all signs of the righteous ardenaline junkie. Switek loomed over his partner; used to dodging and jiving, they were both distinctly uncomfortable since Eddie Rivera, one of their own, had bitten the big one. They tossed up their usual façade of indifference, watching the scurry of activity around them with a detached kind of concern.

At last, Lou Rodriguez roared up in an unmarked official car, giving Switek and Zito something to do.

No matter what Rodriguez did about his wardrobe, he always looked like an unmade bed. His pants were always a shade too short, his shirts a size too big, and his clothing seemed afflicted by a permanent slouch. He'd begun losing hair at thirty-five, and the coffee down at Division had permanently yellowed his teeth. Typically, the vice lieutenant snapped orders and listened to answers with one ear recording information elsewhere. He was a no-nonsense hump-buster of legendary status within the department. His green Dacron jacket hung off him as though subjected to a humidifier and his tie was at half-mast, as usual. One end of his mouth mangled an unlit cigar stub. His eyes darted first to the bomb squad crew, still going over the wreckage of the Chevy with bomb-sniffing dogs, then to Switek and Zito.

Zito nodded towards the burned-out hulk. 'Their guess is C4 plastic explosives, Lieutenant. Rigged to the trunk lock on a tension trip.'

'At least six keys of yap serum went up with Eddie,' said Switek, just as one of the bomb dogs cut loose a wet, wide-bore doggy sneeze. He chuckled, then caught Rodriguez' dead glare and stifled. 'Those mutts'll be up for the next three weeks.'

Zito jumped in before thought could stop him. 'Yeah, watchin' the late show and jackin' up the phone bill, huh?'

'You guys have got a sick sense of humour,' said Rodriguez, without inflection. 'Where's Crockett?'

'In the SID van,' said Switek, nodding in the right direction. 'He's pretty shook up about Eddie.'

Rodriguez moved away. 'You guys oughta be, too.' He left Switek biting his lip, and Zito with his usual out-of-tune expression.

Crockett sat in the van's passenger seat, an unfiltered Lucky Strike dangling from his lips, his eyes set in infinity focus. Rodriguez leaned through the window and lit the smoke for him. Then he climbed into the driver's seat to hear Crockett's version.

Crockett was a pro. 'Four days ago,' he said in a straight monotone, 'I got a line on Corky Fowler, the kid who got vaporized back there. He was a runner for this Puerto Rican named Leon Spangles. Leon works for the Columbian. I played the middleman; told them I had a heavy buyer from LA – Eddie.'

Crockett still could not believe what had happened, how this minor-league bust had abruptly screwed up his whole life. He kept running the details over and over in his mind, as if he might revise them somehow, change the story in the telling so that it left Eddie alive.

'They'd already gotten the word I was a legit runner with a fast boat down at the Marina. Once Eddie flashed the cash, Corky and I were to make the pickup from a Panamanian shrimper eight miles off Bal Harbor.'

Rodriguez' eyes kept straying back to the smouldering junkpile. 'Long way from Bal Harbor, Sonny...'

'Corky showed up today without Leon. Said he'd found a new pipeline, which means he'd cut out the Columbian. He wanted to go into business for himself –'

At the mention of the Columbian, Rodriguez blew a breath of disgust out between his teeth. 'What makes you so sure that this *ghost* you've been chasing for two months, this so-called Columbian drug king, was behind *this*?'

Crockett spat out his smoke. 'For God's sake, Lou! Corky was on the Columbian's payroll and he decided to go it alone! Who the hell *else* would it be? Corky was too

30

small-time to pester anyone on the outside!'

They both sat in the van, simmering, for a full thirty seconds before either of them spoke again. Finally, Rodriguez muttered, 'Still a hot dog, Sonny.'

'Listen, Lou – '

'No! *You* listen!' He cut Crockett off with a chopping motion of his hand. 'This isn't a football game, superstar! I haven't heard word one from you for a whole stinking week! No case reviews, no updates, not a shred of –'

'I was *under*, Lou, setting it up, you know bloody well what –'

'. . . no progress reports, no requests for backup units on the bust –'

Crockett overrode his superior, jerking his thumb viciously towards the alley where Switek and Zito were loitering. 'The *last* time I requested backup, I nearly got shot to death by Bluto and Lee Harvey Oswald over there! And as for progress reports, hell, I'd just as soon buy radio time!' His throat was getting raw from all the yelling.

Rodriguez nailed him with an accusatory look. 'Are you implying that I have a bad cop in my department?'

Crockett didn't know whether to be disgusted or apologetic. He finally decided it wouldn't do any good to tick Lou off. 'All I know is that every time I've gotten within twenty blocks of this Columbian, I've had the pavement yanked right out from under me. Three times running, Lou, and I've never gotten closer than a third-generation contact. Why don't *you* tell *me* that doesn't stink like week-old fish?'

'By the book, Sonny.' It was clear Rodriguez had provided his own solution. 'By the *book*, from here on in, or I swear I'll pull you off the streets. No confiscated speed-boat, no designer threads, no sports-car. Maybe a couple of months driving to a desk job in a '65 Dodge Dart will teach you what being a team player's all about.'

Since Lou had already gotten around to speech-making, Crockett knew he was free to go, for the moment. He booted open the van door. At the sound of a wolf whistle or two he guessed that Gina had arrived on the scene.

He glanced towards the curious Latino crowd corralled behind the police barricades, and saw two women elbowing their way past. The first one to burst past the ribbon was a tall, leggy Italian in high-heeled roughout boots. Her painfully tight hot pants and tied-off blouse showed off enough perfect olive skin to incite a minor urban riot, and she possessed a fabulous cloud of billowing black hair. That was Gina Calabrese.

'Vice, you idiot,' she spat, waving her badge at the first cop who tried to restrain her.

Hot on her trail was Trudy Joplin, another female vice officer working the hooker scam. Both of them had that smooth, slightly weary middle-twenties look. Trudy had mellow, Ethiopian features; she was not so much black as the colour of *café creme*. Working girls, thought Crockett. Of the two he favoured Gina. Trudy walked over to talk to Rodriguez, and as soon as Gina spotted Crockett, he let her come to him.

He began wandering away from the wasted Chevy, and she caught up with him.

'Hi.'

'Hi.' They walked. He shoved his hands into his pockets and watched his feet move. He didn't like making Gina uncomfortable, but just now he felt like hell, and he had to salvage himself before he could be considerate to anyone else.

'I heard about it on the police band,' she said. 'I'm

really sorry, Sonny . . .'

What was the point at which you decided to continue living, after being slugged in the guts by a disaster? Crockett couldn't tell. After a nervy silence, he tried. 'You free for a drink afterwards?'

'Sonny, I – '

'I could really use the company tonight.'

She was honestly apologetic. 'I'm working tonight. I can't get out of it.' The same rules that applied to Sonny governed Gina. She was one of the few women he knew who could fully understand the demands of his job. Maybe that was why he was so powerfully attracted to her; she was his first serious female interest since Caroline. So far, he'd gotten a gentle but firm rebuff. He was guiltily aware that her sympathy for him in the wake of Eddie's death might help erode her apparent resolve not to go out with him, but at the same time he could not deny that their mutual calling came first, with both of them. He felt she wasn't using the job as an excuse, not this time.

He didn't want to make small talk. 'I'll see you around, then. There's something I've got to go do.'

She was about to ask him what, then she realized, and her jaw sagged in dread.

He appeared in the glassed entrance-way of the El Pollo Diner, clothes still grubby from the explosion, the beard stubble on his face making him look like one of the living dead. When he peered in, he instantly saw Maria Rivera.

Her left arm had developed a formidable biceps, from juggling trays, and she hefted one such load and ran the gauntlet of window booths, dropping off a dessert at one, two menus at the second, and a check at the third. Then she set a still steaming Number Four Dinner

Special down in front of a burly Hispanic in gas station coveralls.

'What's this, Maria? The diet plate?'

It was a daily routine between them. To the patrons in the next booth, Maria said, 'Rudolpho's what you call a light eater.' She pulled a pencil down from behind one ear and pointed with it. 'As soon as it gets light, he starts *eating*.' The regulars guffawed and applauded.

She scribbled down an order for burgers and coffee, then looked up to see Sonny by the cigarette machine, pale, drawn, and awkward.

'Hi, Sonny,' she said with genuine friendliness. She and Eddie and Sonny had done the town twenty or thirty times. He'd eaten dinner at their apartment. When Eddie had first announced Maria's pregnancy, Sonny had coughed up a bottle of Dom Perignon, to be drunk the night of the birth.

He swallowed hard as she rushed over to him, still smiling.

'*Qué pasa?*' she said.

## 3

The girl on the T-shaped stage strutted her stuff, hip-bumping and pelvis-grinding, jerking and undulating to the thrumming backbeat. Several bills were already tucked into her silken G-string by the sweatily frantic patrons nearest to the stage. She stomped around on seven-inch spikes with straps, without a wobble and never missing the beat. She had on little else besides the shoes, the G-string, and a ragged leather top that was about to go flying into the faces of her drunken admirers. But first, she thought she might try to coax an offering out of the gyrating black guy next to the head of the ramp.

He was having himself a fine old time.

'*Oh no! Oh no!*' he chanted along with the overamplified playback of Eddie Grant's 'Electric Avenue'. He hustled along in a white suit of raw silk, a five-alarm flammable patterned shirt depicting Snow White and the Seven Samurai, and leather mocs. The shirt was open to the sternum and freed up four or five grand's worth of tacky disco gold. Three pimp-sized diamonds adorned each hand; one hand stayed clamped around a half-consumed stinger. '*We gonna walk! down! to! Electric Avenooo! And 'den we take you higha* – ! Oh, hurt me, mama, hurt me!'

She gave him back a saucy smile and a few more strategic thrusts. Working her way through college, he thought, yeah, sure.

Scotty Wheeler strolled into the club and drank up the scene. Martine, he saw, was doing the cardiac arrest number onstage tonight, and Mickey was behind the bar. He casually drifted towards the latter. Scotty was a barrel-chested man with sandy, curly hair and a regular-guy expression. The barman's eyes lit up with recognition.

'Hey, Lieutenant,' he said. Nobody else could hear him. 'What'll it be? Scotch, rocks?'

Scotty nodded and the bartender poured. When he scooted the glass across, he added, 'The guy in the silk suit. Jamaican. Been in here three nights running, trying to score.'

Scotty sipped and pondered. 'The one dancin' around?'

'Yeah.'

Without a lull, the tape went into 'Somebody's Watching Me', paranoiac-delusional lyrics about being in the twilight zone. The Jamaican and Martine kept boogie-ing away. Scotty slid off his stool and approached the guy from behind.

'Hey, twinkletoes.'

Without looking around, the Jamaican shouted, 'Yeah, mon?' in between lyrics.

'We have to have a little heart-to-heart.' He clapped a catcher's-mitt-sized paw on the black man's shoulder.

'Be with you in a minnit, mon.' He flashed a thousand-dollar smile up at the stripper, and she obliged by shoving her flank in his face. He slipped a C-note into the G-string and her oval eyes widened appreciably. 'Keep up the good work, Princess!' He left her to reach new heights of artistic expression as he followed Wheeler to a private table.

Scotty decided to put the guy on the defensive and

keep him there. 'This . . . *guy* you say you're looking for. What do you want with him?'

'I was told to see Calderone. You know him?'

'Do you?'

'He's a friend of a friend – used to supply merchandise to the friend who supplied me.'

'Used to?'

'Dere was a bust in New York. Three weeks ago. My friend got blown away.' He slugged down some more of his drink. 'You know?'

Scotty gave him his best fed-up, big-deal grimace. 'So the entire state of New York is minus one lousy supplier. So what? Take your bar jive back up to Brooklyn, Rastus. You're outta your league.' He rose from his seat.

The Jamaican's arm shot out to restrain him. 'Hey, *listen*, mon – I can handle four times the weight dat my friend could. I got two hundred grand in my shaving kit, and unlimited resources in New York City . . . hmm?'

Scotty sensed he had this guy on the hook; now to play him a bit. 'Excuse me while I catch my breath.' He glanced at his watch. 'I got a birthday party to go to.'

The Jamaican pushed it another notch. 'Tell him it's Teddy Prentiss – Tooney's friend. He'll know me for sure.' He flipped over a coaster and scribbled down a phone number. Scotty accepted it with just the right touch of reluctance. 'I'll be at this number 'til late tomorrow night. No longer.'

'Well, I'll see what we can do to accommodate you . . . Prentiss.' He turned and lumbered out.

The Jamaican did not return to sample Martine's charms. He watched Scotty very carefully, intensely, as he left the club.

'Where the hell is Daddy?'

'Darling, don't talk like that, please?' Caroline Crockett rarely heard that plaintive, whining tone come into Billy's voice anymore – he was a pretty self-sufficient little six-year-old, and she was proud of him. Occasionally, though, his Daddy's less than sterling habits of language crept into the boy's speech, usually timed just right, to make Mommy jump a bit. Tonight, though, it seemed justified. It was nearly nine-thirty and Sonny had not shown up for his only son's birthday party.

She poured herself a stiff shot of lemonade from the pitcher on the dining-room table. The room was festooned with the debris of a grade-school level birthday blowout, and the dining area had been summarily sacked and abandoned for the living room, where all the presents got a thorough going-over, amid the savaged remnants of wrapping paper, by Billy's gang of pals, which included Donna Wheeler's two kids.

Donna manoeuvred around the gaily-coloured paper shards and boxes, and lifted another lemonade in a toast to Caroline. 'I pronounce this birthday a success,' she said.

From the other side of the dining room, Scotty Wheeler, still decked out in the casual clothes he'd worn to the club that afternoon, added, 'And many many more.'

'Oh my God, don't say that,' Caroline returned, rolling her eyes in consideration of the set-up and clean-up. One very obviously reserved piece of cake remained on the serving platter, surrounded by crumbs. It was as much an accusation as anything Caroline could come up with.

*Once*, she thought, *a long long time ago, you were prettier than any cheerleader, kiddo. And the guys fell all over themselves to get into the same time-zone with you.*

*You had your pick. You picked Sonny Crockett. There's some kind of basic breakdown of logic there, somewhere . . .* In truth, Caroline wore the rigours of motherhood plus a full-time job well; neither had detracted from her resilient Southern beauty. She was from good, venerable Alabama stock. And once upon a time she had been in love with a man named James Crockett – 'Sonny', to his intimates – thereby violating her mother's informal rule that a woman should never marry a football player. Even an ex-football player.

'Hey,' she said to Billy. 'Bobby's taking over your *Planet Destroyer*, chief.'

Billy dashed back into the living room, where Bobby Wheeler was joysticking the new video game from his wheelchair. He had already obliterated most of a galaxy.

Scotty sensed Caroline's pique, and tried to be diplomatic. 'Something must've come up, Caroline – you know how Vice is. This comes with the territory.'

This drew a reproachful look from Donna, who was getting ready to pack her brood up for home and bed.

'Yeah,' said Caroline, still pissed off. 'I know the territory, all right.'

When the doorbell rang, they all froze like murderers caught in the act. Caroline nearly ran to the door, causing Donna to think, *Maybe this divorce isn't gonna work out.*

It was Sonny – or what was left of him – cradling a huge, foil-wrapped gift in one arm. His hair was askew, his clothing still bore the aftermath of the exploding Chevy, and his breath nearly knocked Caroline into the next room. He seemed in perfect control, but a little dazed. Billy's spirits instantly skyrocketed, and he sprang into the air at a run, leaping directly into Sonny's free-arm catch.

'Hi, Dad!'

'Hi, kiddo – how's my boy?'

Billy cocked his head and raised one eyebrow, exaggeratedly. It was a comeback he'd picked up from his dear old dad, and Caroline recognized it immediately.

'How come you're so late?'

Softly, almost soberly, Sonny said, 'I'm sorry, son – I didn't mean to be. But look what I found out on the front lawn with your name written on it.'

Billy dropped down and grabbed the box. 'Can I open it?'

'Right here, right now.'

It was the conflicting emotions she felt that Caroline hated the most. Sonny was a beast, showing up late, only marginally sober, and looking like he'd been mowed down by a tank. But Billy loved his dad so much, without reservation . . . while her own reservations were a little too well known.

Scotty ambled over while Billy dragged his booty into the living room to undergo the scrutiny and approval of his friends.

'Hey man, what's with you – you're half in the bag, for God's sakes.'

Sonny let him finish, then said, 'Eddie Rivera got himself killed today. On a deal I set up.' He said it mostly to the floor.

'Oh, wow!' came Billy's voice from the next room. 'A po-*leese* car! Thanks, Dad!' He came roaring back, clutching a two-foot long, gumball-flashing Dade Metro squad car, and demanded another hug. Sonny held his son tightly, eyes squeezed shut.

Later, after the guests had packed off and the party fallout had been swept to one side, Caroline brewed coffee, and sat with Sonny at the breakfast bar. He wasn't saying much. She had been exhausted by her

40

own day and had no one to tell about it, but she wasn't thinking about that at the moment. She was now too busy trying to kick her tired mind into drawing Sonny out.

He killed off half a cupful and then said, 'Caroline, you suppose if I'd been in some other line of work... things would be different?'

She knew him better than anyone, perhaps too well. 'Doing what?' The thought brought a small smile to her face. 'Dealing real estate? Hot dog vendor? Selling Porsches for my effete brother, downtown?' She almost reached for his hand; had to stop herself. 'You're a cop, Sonny. You'd've hated yourself for giving that up. And if I'd've made you give it up, you would've started hating me.'

He moved with a heavy gait over to the sofa, cleared away a wadded ball of wrapping paper. She sat down with him without being beckoned.

'Been taking an informal survey of my unit this week, marriage-wise,' he said. 'Seems outta sixteen vice cops, we're barely batting two-fifty.'

It was a new variant on an old argument of theirs. 'It's *not* the job, Sonny. Oh, sure – the job has a lot to do with it. Like watching you get shot that time. Waiting alone in bed for one of those phone calls in the dead of night. Those undercover scams that make you vanish for days at a stretch. Your drinking...'

'Gee, darlin', don't sugarcoat it – say what you mean.'

'Since the separation, I've done a lot of thinking,' Caroline said reflectively. 'It's funny, you know. In a lot of ways, you and your vice cop buddies are just the flip side of the same coin as these dealers you're always playing masquerade with...'

This prompted a parallel thought train in Sonny, and he started ruminating before Caroline had finished.

41

'Actually, I think I'm dealing with that kind of pressure better now than I ever have. Compared to when I first started, in plainclothes...' Then he became aware of what Caroline was saying, aware of his shoddy appearance as a direct contradiction to what he was trying to say. Was she telling him that he couldn't separate his job from his life? Wearily, he cut her off with, 'Honey, I'm not in the mood for a psychoanalytic session right now, y'know?'

Caroline folded her arms – she'd always done that, especially when she shifted into her mommy gear and needed to put down the foot of authority. But there was no indictment in her tone, merely understanding. 'You're all players, Sonny. You get high on the action. Even Scotty the family man.'

That seemed to signal an end to the evening. He wanted to hold her in his arms so badly that his stomach hurt... or was it just the Jack Daniels he'd slugged down at his impromptu one-man wake for Eddie?

'I want to look in on Billy,' he said. 'Just for a second. Then I'm gone.'

Caroline bustled, compulsively straightening things in the dining room that did not require neatening. 'Um... you're welcome to spend the night.'

He looked at her and their eyes held for a beat too long. She found herself in the awkward position of having to specify, 'I'll make up the couch.' She didn't want him driving in the shape he was in.

There were too many past moments between them. Sonny smiled a brutal, private smile. He'd decline. She listened to his footsteps as he wound back towards Billy's room.

Caroline continued her clean-up campaign without any real direction, until she looked at the clock and noticed Sonny had been gone for ten minutes. A bit skittishly she checked, half-expecting to find him waiting for her in what used to be their shared bed. *Wouldn't that be a kick, after all we've gone through?* she thought.

But Sonny was still in Billy's room. She heard him snoring, softly. In the dim glow of Billy's Spiderman night light she saw them, Big Crockett and Little Crockett, Sonny hanging partially off the tiny bed, fast asleep, with Billy snuggled irremovably into his embrace.

Her throat clogged fast after that. She brought her hand up just in time to intercept the single tear that found its way past her defences.

Leon de Santis made sure everybody noticed as he rolled up to the club outside Nunzio's Cuban Bar-be-Q in Española, standing on the brakes and sliding into the parking slot like a hand into a glove in front of the rubber burn-marks he left on the street. Leon has arrived, he thought. His vintage DeLorean instantly attracted the notice of a pair of Latino streetwalkers, and after he jumped out he gave them a courtly bow. 'Top 'o' the afternoon, ladies,' he grinned, exposing gold-lined teeth. All he really wanted was a bucket of Nunzio's fabulous BBQ ribs.

When he boogie-ed out of the bar, he failed to notice the gleaming black '84 Corvette slotted in behind his own car. As soon as he sat down in the pilot bucket, he was joined by Sonny Crockett, who slammed the door of the DeLorean hard. Irritation flashed across Leon's ebony features, but he recovered nicely.

'Feed your face later, Leon,' said Sonny. 'You and I are going to take a lap around the block together.'

Leon slapped on his usual mask of superior disdain and tore off a hunk of orange meat with his perfect teeth.

Chomp, chomp. He looked utterly bored. 'Some other time, Burnett. I'm a little *hongry*, y'know?'

Crockett's eyes went hard and silver. He slapped the food out of Leon's mitt and it splattered between the low seats of the custom sports car. Continuing the violent movement, he jerked a dull grey .45 automatic free from his armpit and shoved the muzzle into Leon's ribcage hard enough to make the gangly black man grunt. 'Why put off till tomorrow what we can do today?' he hissed.

Leon was smart enough to realize Crockett was on a hair trigger, and was himself a study in cool as he set down the bucket, stuck the keys into the ignition, and drove as instructed. He hated losing face, though, and started up again soon enough. 'You must be crazy, Burnett. You barge into my *car*, slap barbeque sauce all over my *upholstery* . . . jeez, I've *killed* people for less –'

'Spare me the tough talk, Leon. You and the Columbian have already made your dead body quota for the month – car bomb, late yesterday, 59th Street underpass?'

He shot Crockett a flinty, disbelieving look, and shook his head. 'People get killed all the time in this town trying to go inta business for them*selfs*, so lighten up and get your cannon away from my appendix, Jack.'

Crockett cocked the hammer. 'You *also* blew away my end of a two hundred thousand dollar deal, spongehead. Now you tell the Columbian I wanna meet with him. About my commission.'

Leon kept his eyes on the road. He reached down and tried to slap the gun away. 'Hey, dammit! I've seen the man put together twenty *million* dollar deals, Burnett – and I ain't talking just *once*, neither. There's no way the man is gonna meet with *you*.' He eyed Crockett's clothes. 'Unless you – hah! – up your status a bit. Who gives a damn about that nickel and dime jive?' He pulled up alongside Crockett's Corvette – another job bonus, by virtue of the impound boys. 'Once around the block, great white chief. Anything else I can do ya for?'

When Crockett stowed the gun, Leon seemed to get a blast of sudden insight. While checking out his orthodonture in the rearview, he added, 'Tell you what I'll do, Burnett. Forget about Corky and that wimp from Malibu. Your original deal with me is still open – just 'cause I like you.'

Crockett wanted to throw up. The smell of the ribs wasn't doing his hangover an ounce of good. 'You got a shipment coming in?'

'Tonight. Ten grand for you and your speedboat. One hour max, pickup *and* delivery.' When this failed to thaw Crockett's icy expression, he added, by way of apology, 'Look, man, I'm sorry about your client and all, but that bomb weren't meant for nobody but Corky, that spaced-out little speed freak. Then again, there's *always* buyers.'

Crockett was right back where he'd started in more ways than one. 'Where and when?'

'Indian creek. Midnight. Want some ribs?'

'Snort the damned ribs, Leon.' He slammed the car door again.

Leon winced. Some dudes had no respect for the craftsmanship success could buy.

## 4

Crockett's cigarette boat was a state-of-the-art contraband runner, all streamlined fibreglass and growling Merc V-1750 dual powerhouses, worth ten times his commission for this night's labours. Crockett was wearing his black T-shirt and Levis; Leon lounged his lanky frame in the co-pilot couch and occasionally peered ahead to give directions. The water was as black as an oil slick and the speedboat's running lights were down. Crockett manoeuvred the monster between other moored ships at a healthy thirty or so. Off in the nighttime distance was Miami Beach, all noise and lights and carnival atmosphere.

'Up ahead,' pointed Leon. 'On the left.' He talked very little when there was actually a deal going down.

Crockett cut to quarter-throttle and glided towards a barely visible dock, jutting darkly into the sea. To the north, an enormous cargo ship, the *Star of Egypt*, grew up into the night, silent and looming. Near the head of the dock he could see a parked Cadillac El Dorado in fire-engine red, and two figures, one large and formidable, the other wiry, standing in wait.

'Little guy's the Jamaican,' said Leon. Crockett could see the silhouetted figure held a briefcase.

The larger one guided Crockett in using a masked flashlight. Crockett and Leon quickly and efficiently moored the boat and jumped off. The group converged on the middle of the short little pier.

Crockett expertly concealed his surprise at seeing Scotty Wheeler again so soon. The Jamaican, he didn't know. Leon was in the lead and doing the dealing. 'You got the cash?'

The Jamaican, Teddy Prentiss, hefted the briefcase. 'One hundred and twenty thousand, mon. You got the party favours?'

'Three kilos of love dust in the boat.'

The Jamaican nodded, understanding that he was to go get it out of the boat himself. He had time to make a single step before the whole neighbourhood came alive with red lights.

Four undercover cars, magnetic bubbles and sirens blaring in an all-out, epileptic-seizure Code Three, came slewing and smoking off Collins Avenue and cut off the El Dorado. Scotty and Crockett, playing out their roles, immediately put their hands on their heads, fingers interlaced, assuming the classical position. Leon and Teddy Prentiss nearly collided in panic, Leon heading for the shore with his long, loping strides; Prentiss bashing roughly into Crockett and then making tracks for the cigarette boat.

'Who sent you an invitation?' Crockett said to Wheeler, beneath all the immediate panic.

'Since when do I need an invite to my own party?' he said sardonically. 'I only dug up the Jamaican yesterday.'

Among the narcs running up, hoglegs drawn, were Switek and Zito, eager to be visible now that it was clear there wouldn't be any shooting. 'Hands on heads, sleazeballs!' Switek barked, and Sonny nearly burst out laughing.

Over his shoulder, Scotty watched the Jamaican leap into the boat. 'Sure hope you took the keys out of that monster.'

'Come on, Scott, who do you think you're dealing with, here?' He dropped his hands to pat his back pocket, expecting the reassuring jingle of the keys. No go.

The twin Mercs fired into life behind them.

'I'm talkin' to a guy that's about to lose a hundred grand's worth of speedboat,' said Scotty.

The colour drained out of Crockett's face. 'Like hell!' He lit out for Zito's car, a white Camaro with a red racing stripe, because he knew the keys would still be in it. When he burst between the two he nearly knocked Zito off into the water. 'A little *early*, aren'tcha, airheads!'

The 'bust', such as it was, still hadn't been completed. 'Sonny,' Switek said, affronted, 'you're not supposed to –'

But Sonny was already wasting Zito's steel-belted Tiger Paws getting back onto Collins Avenue, hitting sixty before reaching the pavement in order to parallel-chase the cigarette boat along the shoreline.

Keeping the boat in sight and not centre-punching the oncoming traffic, with the glare from the street-lamps reducing visibility, was proving to be partically impossible. Crockett was thankful he knew the contours of his own boat so well, and hoped the Jamaican wasn't as familiar with the local waterways.

In the boat, the Jamaican rammed it up to full throttle and was smashed back into the pilot's chair as the boat demonstrated its top speed. The prow rose from the water, the dual Mercs roared, gobbling gasoline, and the coastline started flying by in fast-motion. Teddy Prentiss was scared but delighted, thrilling to the kidney-wrenching momentum, shouting into the blitz of oncoming wind. 'You *beast*, you!' he bellowed at the boat, grinning.

The hindquarters of a top-heavy Winnebago swayed in Sonny's immediate path just as the cigarette boat poured on the speed. Now he was bristling. He mashed down the pedal and soared over into the opposing lane. Motorists honked and screeched and finally swerved from his target path, taking out mailboxes, newspaper vending machines and the decorative palms dotting the centre strip. Sonny kept pace with the speedboat until he had to tuck the Camaro back into the far lane to avoid a supermarket semi that gave him a shot on the diesel horn but did not evade. Then a Metro busload of people obstructed his path. Sonny cursed and cranked hard right, skidding into a row of parked cars and shearing away their door handles and mirrors on the streetward side.

He'd lost sight of the boat. Somewhere a police siren was already whooping, bearing down on the accident scene. If he stayed on Collins, he'd wind up flattening pedestrians in the heart of Miami.

Prentiss watched the Camaro's predicament and laughed. If he had turned and noticed the tugboat wallowing in front of him a second later, he and the cigarette boat would have been a messy headline and little more. Opting not to explode at seventy miles per hour, he took the boat into a panic turn that nearly capsized him.

Then he spotted a narrow intercoastal waterway that wound away from the coastline. The Camaro could not follow him into the water, so he dropped speed and helmed the craft into the little canal, sensing his pursuer fuming, tied to the roadway back there.

All Crockett saw was a hint of the stern being swallowed by darkness. The Camaro nosed streetward as he brought it to an angry stop, bouncing his fist off the dash in frustration. About a mile down, he remembered, there was a railroad trestle spanning Indian Creek. Prentiss would have to pass right under it.

Crockett gunned the car. There were still a few speeding laws he hadn't broken yet, and he'd need to flaunt them righteously in order to beat the boat to the trestle.

Prentiss had slowed the boat to a crawl. Other ships and weird-looking construction equipment was barely discernible in the pitch darkness; he didn't want to chance ramming into something fatal before he'd used up the boat. He tried to make his eyes widen, to see better in the absence of light. He must be in a shipyard, or something, he thought. It was like a back alley with water instead of pavement.

He peered down, around... up...

The Camaro sat forty feet above him, pieces of its suspension still dropping off from the mad dash across the railyard. It was parked on a service bridge. That was all he could register before Crockett's airborne mass blacked everything out.

Crockett dropped and hit the black man high on the shoulder blades. Together they pitched over the helm, scrabbling for control. Prentiss was wearing a silk tie; Crockett grabbed it and swung a fist wildly towards the face that had to be above the knot. But the other man's fist hit him first. Lightning scattered across Crockett's inner eyelids and he floundered backwards.

When he opened his eyes, Prentiss was dragging out a pistol.

Crockett punched the throttle, causing the cigarette boat to lurch in the water. He hung onto the backrest and kicked Prentiss' gun, hard. His hand sprang open and the .357 pistol cartwheeled over the side, unfired, making a pathetic little splash when it hit the water.

Crockett pulled up his own automatic. The first cartridge was already chambered, so all he had to do was cock it to calm his oppenent down. The engine of the cigarette boat thrummed beneath them.

Hating protocol more than ever, he dug out his shield, as he was required to. 'Freeze it solid' he said. 'Miami Vice.'

The black man's mouth dropped open. Then Crockett encountered a reaction he'd never seen before on a bust. Was it relief he read on the face of Teddy Prentiss, even a degree of ironic humour?

When his hand moved again for his breast pocket, Crockett motioned with the gun. 'Watch it. Real slow.' Deliberately, with experienced calm, the Jamaican's hand drew out an object quite familiar to Sonny – a badge wallet.

'Tubbs,' the black man said, displaying his own shield. 'NYPD. Congratulations, pal.' Then it was Sonny's turn to gape.

Crockett wanted to break something, bad. He couldn't throw the coffee cups in the Northeast Miami Metro Station; they were all styrofoam. He finally settled for crushing one into a shapeless ball after draining it. He hated styrofoam. It imparted a pasty taste to the precinct house's already lethal brew. It didn't retain a pleasingly mutilated appearance when you savaged it in anger. It had no weight. When Crockett pitched it disgustedly towards the nearest bin, it caught an air current and settled to the dirty tile floor halfway between his feet and the trashcan.

Lou Rodriguez and Detective Tubbs looked at Sonny warily.

'Two weeks!' he yelled, attracting the passing notice of the other cops and their catches of the evening. 'Two friggin' *weeks* I've put in on busting Leon, and three fourths of the dealers at the bust turn out to be cops! Me, Scotty Wheeler, and Doctor Voodoo here, putting in a *surprise* guest appearance, direct from Fun City!' Tubbs didn't flinch. 'How come I wasn't told about Scotty, Lou? How come Heckle and Jekyll jumped the gun and brought in the cavalry five bloody minutes *early*?'

'Yeah,' said Rodriguez, 'I'm aware of that, but –'

Crockett overrode him. 'That what you mean by team playing, Lou?'

'What I'm trying to tell you is that they were to *foul up* the bust so that Leon –'

'You know, Lou, my badge says 'Miami' but lately it's been looking an awful lot like Disney World!'

'*Shut up*, Crockett!' Sonny had been beefing and moaning ever since the wrapup, and Lou felt the detective had just reached the limit of his leash. 'Tubbs is here on priority clearance, per direct request of the NYPD. *Interagency memo*, Crockett – confidential. You dig?'

Calmly, with a clear sense of the upper hand, Tubbs put in, 'And I'd kinda like to keep it that way, if you catch my drift. *Mon*.' His Jamaican accent had magically evaporated in favour of his native Bronx lilt. 'No offence, but when it comes to security leaks, Miami ain't exactly Pentagon South.'

That stopped Crockett, who glared at Lou victoriously. 'Interesting perspective.' Lou shifted around and Crockett refocused on the black man. 'So tell me now, Butts –'

'Tubbs.' He kept cool. 'My friends call me Raphael.'

'You down here for some *specific* value to the

taxpayers, or you just workin' on your tan?'

Tubbs laughed. It was a nasty sound, and there was no humour in his eyes. 'Such mirth! One o'clock in the morning and the man hands out zingers for free!' It was quite likely that he might attack Sonny and bestow a bloody lip on the smart mouth.

Rodriguez held up his hands to try and force a truce. Tubbs sniffed and continued. 'Ever hear of a dealer named Francisco Calderone?'

Crockett shrugged.

'About a month ago one of our detectives set up a meet with Calderone and a New York pusher named Tooney. Big stakes. The bust went ... sour. Our boy and his partner got massacred. We took out Tooney, but Calderone got away. He split New York faster than you could sneeze.'

'NYPD figures he's down here,' said Lou.

Crockett's body language made it evident his time was being squandered. 'He's here alongside five thousand other pony league pushers with five aliases each and passports to match. Big deal.'

'He killed a cop.'

'Slightly bigger deal.'

Tubbs stayed at a low boil. 'The dude I showed up with tonight was one of his front men. I was setting him up for a rollover when that trained monkey act of yours dropped out of the trees.'

'That was the Switek and Zito Travelling Medicine Circus and Brass Band,' chuckled Crockett. 'I figured they'd impress a worldly urban law enforcement officer such as yourself ... whatever you said your name was.' The hostility was growing less disguised, bubbling nearer to the surface. 'Been in town three days and already he's an expert. That "dude" you connected with, Scotty Wheeler, works for the DEA. And Leon is

53

on the payroll of a Columbian I've been two steps behind for *months* now!'

Nobody jumped into the thudding silence. Tubbs deliberately reached into his breast pocket and drew out a slightly soggy 9×12 photographic blow-up, folded into quarters. The creases broke the coating and made white, fuzzy lines, but interrupted nothing important. 'Surveillance shot, taken before the shoot-out.' He pointed to faces. 'This is Tooney, our man, the back of Jake Bartamas' head, and the guy in the limo is Calderone.'

Crockett blanched. 'The Columbian. I'll be damned.'

Tubbs looked to Rodriguez for details. 'Suspect in a half-dozen drug murders down here. He moves a *lot* of weight. There are few fish bigger. We've never even been able to find out his name.' He turned to Crockett, with a wry and somewhat accusatory expression. 'Looks like you two are after the same man. Instead of pounding on each other, maybe you two oughta consider –'

'Working together?' interposed Crockett. Eddie Rivera had barely been dead twenty-four hours, and he resented Lou shoving this stranger at him as a substitute. 'Forget it. Goodnight, Lou.' He knew what a spectacle he was presenting, slouching out of the precinct room in such a state. He didn't care. The whole night had been a bust, and not the kind he'd wanted. As his parting shot, he stabbed a finger towards the photo Tubbs had produced. 'I'll want a copy of that first thing tomorrow morning, Lou.' For him, Tubbs didn't even exist anymore.

After the door banged shut, Tubbs said to Rodriguez, 'You look a tad amused. Who the hell does that guy think he is?'

## 5

Accustomed to the intensity of Manhattan, Tubbs was unprepared for the atmosphere of Miami. In New York, your blood raced beneath a sky of dull iron-grey. Miami, by contrast, seemed to stand still, baking in the near tropical south-eastern heat. The intensity here was not of pace, but of sheer brightness. Tubbs found he was unable to go outdoors in Miami without hanging sunglasses on his face. New York was a study in flat ink-wash tones; Miami was like staring into a sunlamp and feeling it bake your brains. The surface of the sea glittered harshly, almost painfully, as though a billion silver coins were strewn over it. In the city, the heat was phsyically suffocating.

Tubbs located the Bal Harbor Yacht Basin with no more difficulty than he'd had finding anything else in Miami ... which meant he'd doubled back on the freeway twice to find the right exit. He'd spent an unsatisfactory, mostly sleepless night in his plastic hotel room, the air conditioner cranked up full blast to give him enough background noise to permit him to doze. When he woke up he had the sniffles; he felt absurd blowing his nose constantly when the temperature would hit ninety degrees by ten a.m. In addition to being an interloping outsider, an out-of-towner without portfolio, and a hopeless *turista* on the expressways, he was now a bona fide victim of the climate.

Arranged before him in neat, bobbing rows was a good fifty million dollars' worth of luxury yachts, speedboats and sailing vessels. Rodriguez had told Tubbs to find the mooring space leased to *Burnett*, and after a bit of browsing Tubbs located the *St Vitus Dance*, a thirty-eight-foot exercise in hand-caulked teak decks and conspicuous consumption, ancient but well-tended. Moored alongside it, shrouded in a brown canvas tarp, was the cigarette boat he'd stolen the night before.

Tubbs walked along the dock, giving the boat a once over, while balancing a pink take-out box in one hand. While he admired the vessel – knowing next to *nada* about such things, he assumed what he saw was impressive – Sonny Crockett made his way out of the galley hatch, moving slowly, arthritically, with the careful, gravity-conscious motions of a man who has spent another night in the company of pills and alcohol.

His back was to Tubbs, an opportunity offering itself, irresistibly.

No sooner had Crockett attempted to straighten his spine than Tubbs bellowed, in the loudest possible voice, *'Ensign Tubbs reporting for duty, SIR*!!'

Sonny stiffened and cracked his skull on the main boom. *'Damn* it!' he winced, then looked up to see Tubbs grinning and holding an arrow-straight mock salute. He let his bones collapse into the nearest lounge chair and rubbed his thumping head while Tubbs jumped aboard, balancing his box.

With a sweeping gesture, Tubbs rubbed in some salt. 'Ah, it's a great day to be alive, ain't it, Crockett?'

'Yeah, or to beat somebody to death,' he growled. 'Depending on your disposition. What're you doing out in the white part of town?'

'Here.' Tubbs handed over a manila folder, not

wanting to play the ranking game of insults with Crockett just yet. 'Photocopies of your good friend Señor Calderone, remember? Have some coffee and doughnuts.' He opened the box and the smell of coffee hit Crockett like a tonic. He accepted a steaming paper cupful from Tubbs with a grunt that was almost like gratitude. 'Rodriguez said look for you under the name Burnett. That your cover?'

Crockett glanced at the photocopies and nodded, then dropped them on the deck. 'That's the general idea, *mon*. Far as the locals are concerned, I'm just another hard-partyin' ocean guy of questionable means.'

'With a hundred thousand dollar cigarette boat and a sideline of recreational stimulants.'

'Mm.' Put that way, it sounded outrageous even to Crockett. But life had a way of being outrageous despite his best attempts to make it mundane and boring. He shifted around in his seat, letting the rays of the sun burn off his grogginess, letting the coffee wash away the eye-grating afterburn of last night's pop. 'This cop that bought it up in New York – he an acquaintance of yours?'

'We knew each other,' Tubbs said tightly. It was time for his pitch: 'Listen, man – I was thinking about what Rodriguez said.' No response. 'About us working together on this Calderone thing? I think it's a –'

'Save your breath, Tubbs.' For the first time he looked at him directly, shielding his eyes. 'I got enough problems with this investigation already without playing tour guide to some wide-eyed understudy down here on a weekend pass.'

'Wait a second –'

'No, *you* wait a second!' Crockett rose and dumped the coffee overboard. 'You might have commendations up the kazoo in the Bronx or New York or wherever the hell it is you're from, but this is *Miami*, pal, where you can't tell the players with or with*out* a scorecard! That little fiasco last night should've proved that down here you're just another amateur. A *slow* amateur, at that.' He grinned maliciously to himself.

Tubbs moved with him, staying in his line of fire, determined not to be cut off again by another of Crockett's high-volume interruptions. 'Yeah, slow enough to steal the keys to your damned boat right outta your back pocket while you stood there on the dock like a zombie last night! And what are you, Crockett-Burnett, God's supreme gift to law enforcement?' They were glaring at each other now, adversarially, the two meanest cats in the alley. 'Excuse me if I don't break down in disappointment, but from what *I* hear, your yin-yang is fulla suspensions for misconduct, not to mention car bombs, which means you ain't the *safest* guy in the world to be teamed up wi –'

Crockett did not cut in. He pivoted and punched Tubbs right in the jaw. Tubbs' arms windmilled and he plonked solidly down, right on the teakettle, dazed and cross-eyed. Finally, the ocean-front came back into focus and he massaged his jaw. 'Guess I went and asked for that one, huh?'

Crockett was angry, but mostly over his own loss of control. Tubbs had handily gotten right under his skin, and prodded the place that hurt. He looked a bit disgusted with himself. First Caroline, then Eddie, now this stranger from New York, who looked like Rufus from 'Doonesbury', all grown up. 'You didn't, man. That was totally out of line.'

'You really think so?'

'Absolutely.' He extended his hand to help Tubbs up. Tubbs launched off the deck and coldcocked

Crockett with a Brooklyn back-alley right. Crockett fell over the deck chair and sprawled, coming up with a mixture of amazement and fresh, homicidal anger on his face. 'Couldn't let you handle all that bad karma by yourself,' smiled Tubbs. The smile withered when it stretched his sore jaw. 'Hey – you wouldn't happen to have any ice on this bucket, wouldya?'

The killer glint faded from Sonny's eyes. 'Sure. Down below, help yourself. Bring some back for me.'

Tubbs slid open the galley hatch and peeked into the gloomy darkness below. There was a smell of stale bedding and . . . something else, unidentifiable. His foot found the first step, then the second.

A quarter-second after Tubbs' head ducked in, Crockett watched Tubbs himself come flying up from belowdecks as though drop-kicked, accompanied by a bellowing basso roar that vibrated the entire sloop. Tubbs screamed, heel hooking the step and dumping him on his can. He tried to scrabble backward, crablike, away from the hatch and the monster that had appeared in it.

Crockett laughed.

Tubbs was staring between his knees at the gnarly muzzle of a ten-foot long alligator, whose head would have been the third step down before it snapped at him. The closing jaws looked to Tubbs like a coffin lid shutting the wrong way, and they were chock-full of crooked yellow teeth. The scaly horror bellowed again, a bull-grumble that brought the hair on the back of Tubbs' neck to full parade attention, and it lunged for him, the cavernous maw clamping shut on empty air with a solid *crunk* noise. He then saw that it was restrained by a leash of half-inch industrial chrome chain, wound double around the fat neck.

Crockett righted the deck chair and kicked back,

firing up a Lucky with his Zippo paratrooper's lighter. Before Tubbs could scream again, he said, 'Officer Tubbs, say hello to Elvis – former mascot of the University of Florida football Gators. Currently he's engaged as the watchdog and resident dope-sniffer of *St Vitus Dance*.' Proudly, he winked at the reptile and added, 'He got, um, *benched* his senior year for taking a little chomp out of a Georgia free safety . . .'

Elvis cut loose some more thunder.

Tubbs didn't care how much of Crockett's patter was bull. He was pressed flat and PO'ed. 'Hey – hey – call it off, man, I don't even like alligator *shoes* – !'

Crockett's face went hard. 'Hey, don't talk like that; you're gonna hurt his feelings!' Then he stepped between Tubbs and the creature and hunkered down. Elvis immediately forgot about Tubbs and lifted his huge prow of a head so Crockett could stroke it. 'Don't mind him, Elvis. He's from New York.'

The gutteral growling changed register, to a purr-like thrumming, as Crockett patted the shapeless knob of scale-armoured nose. The golden reptile eyes looked slightly glazed as the creature stared off into space.

Gulping, trying to stand, Tubbs said, 'I'm surprised you don't have a hook for a hand.'

Crockett considered this. 'That Captain Hook trip is strictly for non-herpetologists. Some punks did feed him an alarm clock in '81. He crunched it and passed it. Gators eat more garbage than twenty goats. But I think it gave him a taste for alarm clocks. He's eaten four of mine. He prefers Japanese digitals, I think . . .'

Elvis agreed, with a sound like an idling diesel motor.

Tubbs moved carefully closer. 'Takes a ticking and keeps on licking, huh?'

'Ugh.' Crockett continued petting the beast. 'He's still a little freaked out – he ate a flight bag full of LSD on a Key West lab bust last Thursday. But all in all I feel he's in a much better environment now.'

To Tubbs, this was getting too surreal. He saw Crockett tilt his head to try and read his watch. 'It's time to take Elvis for his walk or something?'

'Nope.' Crockett reached behind Elvis and grabbed a shirt. 'Gotta bail hearing downtown. I got busted last night, remember?'

'You mean "Sonny Burnett" got busted.'

'Yeah. Me and Scotty have got to be there for Leon de Santis' long-awaited debut as a lead vocalist.'

'Ho, dream on. You think Leon's gonna roll over on Calderone after what happened to Corky Fowler? No way.'

'I didn't say anything about him *wanting* to. But he will. The judge has got a surprise up his sleeve. Just stand by, Tubbs, and watch how real law enforcement works.'

'What am I supposed to do while you're at the hearing?' Tubbs knew he couldn't show up; Leon would recognize him as a cop if he did.

'Why don't you stay right here. Feed Elvis his breakfast. Here.' He flipped open a cooler and handed over a large, frozen halibut, tail-first. '*Bon apetit*. If he gets a little uppity, just rub his belly. He loves that.'

'Rub his – ?' He looked nervously at Elvis, who had eyes only for the halibut. Crockett was halfway down the dock, his jacket slung over one shoulder, leaving Tubbs in a Mexican standoff with a ten-foot eating machine that was freaked out on blotter acid flashbacks. 'Uh . . . nice alligator? Damn you, Crockett . . .'

Elvis roared his disapproval. Tubbs jumped reflexively, hurling the fish, which Elvis caught in a vice-like, crunching deathgrip. As he mangled it enough to swallow, his eyes stared on, unblinking, recording weird, reptilian hallucinations while Tubbs stood there tyring to figure out what to do next.

'For God's sake, Monroe, will you *do* something about the climate control in this sweatshop?'

Judge Rupp's voice echoed throughout the hallowed chamber of justice and brought the entire legal machine to a brief halt on account of the sweltering heat, which made the high-ceilinged room feel like the belly of an industrial dryer. Sumner T. Rupp was more commonly known as 'Send-em-up-Rupp', and was a bit of a local legend with his Southern-fried accent, his flyaway silver hair and his butt-busting way with the gavel. Monroe, a court officer, hustled out to try to bring cooler air to all while Rupp swivelled towards the bailiff and thundered, 'Take your *time*, Humphries, I got nothing better to do!'

Humphries snapped out of his trance and automatically read from his clipboard, in a high-school principal monotone. 'Uh – bail proceeding – uh case number 142573, Dade County Municipal uh Court; Leon Abdullah de Santis. Please uh approach the bench.'

Dressed down for the hearing in a simple black three-piece ensemble, Leon rose from the defendants' area and moved forward in the company of a typical drug lawyer – tanned, wearing suede loafers, with harsh gold-rimmed, point-making spectacles – secure in the knowledge that this minor travail would consume no more than five minutes of his valuable time. Near their empty seats were Crockett and Scotty Wheeler, dressed in their wardrobe from the previous night's action, looking for all the world like two weary dope smugglers who had just spent a cheerful night in the slammer flicking roaches off the bunks. Behind them, a multi-ethnic multitude of cheap lawyers, cannibal-rat prosecutors, bailiffs and cops, accused felons and their mommies all fretted and shifted, suffering in the stifling heat.

Crockett leaned to Scotty's ear. 'You turning cowboy on me, Scotty, or were you just giving your backups the night off?'

In an undertone Scotty replied, 'I wasn't planning any bust last night, m'boy, until Switek and Zito stormed in. Your troops, not mine. I wanted to hold off until Leon reported home to the Columbian, and nab them both.' The official-looking document Scotty kept sneaking glances at, Crockett now realized, was a betting sheet.

'Give you seven points and take the Dolphins for an even hundred.'

Scotty grinned. 'A man with a fantasy life. Okay, you're on. I'm gonna have to establish a trust fund in your name.'

Judge Rupp fixed Leon and his legal chickenhawk with a withering Old Testament glare and said, 'In accordance with prior recommendation, Mr de Santis and . . .'

Abruptly, every single light in the courthouse went to black, immersing the room in total darkness.

A booming voice announced: 'One move and you're history, buster.' It was Rupp.

The lights flickered back on, the bar flourescents winking weakly, then charging full. At least ten firearms, from .38 revolvers and police .357s to Remington riot guns, were aimed in a spoke-like circle at Leon. Judge Rupp himself held a sawed-off elk rifle two inches from the skinny black dealer's nostrils. The District Attorney aimed a .44 Magnum. Humphries held a twelve-gauge shotgun with an eight-shot magazine. Martha McGivers, the elderly court reporter, held a nickle-plated Italian automatic, targeted poker-straight to the browless space between Leon's eyes.

Footsteps hurried down the corridor and Monroe burst back into the room. 'A little overload problem on account of the heat, Your Honour.'

Murmurs of relief swept the chamber and most of the firepower was stowed and holstered. Rupp re-sheathed the elk rifle beneath the bench. 'Not exactly a high watermark for our power plant,' he said, as though sermonizing, 'but nevertheless, a glowing testament to our Constitutional right to bear arms!'

Sonny felt his guts twist in mirth, but kept a straight face. Martha McGivers stayed where she was, ready to blow Leon's mug to smithereens if he twitched. Rupp noticed and leaned over the edge of the bench, a succouring, paternal note coming into his voice. 'Put the gun away now, Martha. Martha?'

Martha let the hammer down easy and reseated herself before her machine.

'Now,' said Rupp. 'As per recommendation of the State Attorney's office –'

'Here it comes,' said Sonny, *sotto voce.*

'– and in consideration of your investigative co-operation with that office, I'm hereby waiving all bail and releasing you on your own recognizance pending preliminary hearing...'

Rupp banged the gavel but no one heard it. Crockett was inwardly tickled at the way Leon seemed to lose all colour when he heard what the judge was saying. He saw the dealer's mouth form the words *what cooperation?* and by the time Rupp had finished, Leon was fighting his way towards the bench, pushing off the restraining grasp of his attorney.

'I didn't cooperate with no State Attorney!'

'I'd advise you merely to count your blessings, Mr de Santis,' Rupp said sternly.

'Leon,' said the lawyer urgently, 'what he means is –'

'Shut up! Get outta my face! This dude's gonna get me *killed* talkin' crap like that!'

Rupp banged the gavel again, rising, like Zeus from a throne on Olympus, yelling over Leon's strident protests, 'I said put a lid on it, sir, or I'll personally hold you in contempt of this court – !'

Leon almost made it to the bench before the marshalls hammerlocked him. 'I didn't roll over on *nobody*, Jack! You think I'm insane! I want custody, man, I ain't going outside this building, I ain't going no-damned-place like this here!'

Wheeler caught a conspiratorial glance jumping from the Assistant State Attorney, Gordon Avery, and Crockett. He was about to ask Sonny what the scene was all about when Rupp did his act with the gavel again.

'Next case! Hurry it up, man . . .'

'Bail proceeding 142754,' recited Humphries. 'Sonny T. Burnett, please rise and approach the bench.'

With a lackadaisical shrug, Sonny muttered, 'I'm-innocent-Your-Honour-it-was-all-a-mistake,' and then shuffled towards the bench.


Tubbs watched Leon storm down the courthouse steps three jumps ahead of his attorney, and saw heated words exchanged. As expected, Leon seemed free as a sparrow, but the man did not seem too relieved.

Leon's trajectory would bring him abreast of the Z28 convertible Tubbs had driven out from Bal Harbor, so Tubbs watched and waited. Leon's lawyer was apparently trying to coax him into taking a lift home; Leon kept glancing around the open courtyard with paranoid hypersensitivity, imagining potential assassins behind every lamppost and parked car. Finally, he waved the attorney away and stormed in Tubbs' general direction, nearly bowling over a plump Mexican man. Poor Leon, for some reason unknown to Tubbs, was about to blast off.

Tubbs cranked open the door and stepped out, the kilo of jangling gold around his neck completing his summerweight pimp ensemble. 'Leon!' he barked.

Leon spun as though stabbed from behind, a vision of ultrafine panic nerves, and then recognized Tubbs. He walked towards the Z28 turned to one side, as though he was edging around a building. His eyes were furtive, darting.

'Got a hunnert and twenty grand I b'lieve belongs to your boss, mon,' he said, resuming the Jamaican drawl of his Teddy Prentiss cover. 'You care to *parlez-vous* on that?'

'I don't know you!' Leon nearly screamed. 'What'cha talking about! I don't know nothing!' Then he made tracks away, almost blundering into a sidewalk bicyclist who swerved and swore. He was so freaked he made Elvis seem like a lap dog.

Tubbs let him stack up a bit of distance, then he fired up the engine of the Z28.

## 6

Crockett's Zippo lighter, burnished by decades of wear, had been a gift from his father, who had been a paratrooper during the invasion of Normandy. He dug it out as he watched Lou Rodriguez fumble with a pack of paper matches. Lou looked up and caught him watching.

'Stop looking so damned sure of yourself,' he said. 'And gimme a light.'

Crockett finished pouring out another crummy styrofoam cupload of the Metro Station's killer java. 'Come on, Lou, they practically needed a tow truck to hustle Leon out of the courtroom today.' He leaned over and flicked the wheel of the lighter for Lou to grill his ever-present cigar stub.

'There're no guarantees,' said Lou, puffing. At least the smoke deadened the odour of the coffee.

'Five'll get you ten he's on the horn to us before the hour's up, caterwauling for protective custody and just begging to do anything to help us out. Right, Switek?'

Across the squad room, Switek was hunched over a typewriter, owlishly pecking out a report at about five words a minute. 'Yeah, mmffph,' he said, half a cinnamon doughnut in his yap. 'Put me down for twenty bucks.'

D.A. Avery and Scotty Wheeler – now minus his dealer's getup – entered and picked their way through the usual chaos of the precinct towards Lou and Sonny.

'Hey guys,' said Scotty. 'Avery filled me in on the ride over here. Slick, very slick.' He nodded approvingly.

Sonny cackled fiendishly, enormously pleased with himself. Lou reached out and tugged Scotty's tie with a look of confusion. 'Look at this guy – looks more like an investment counsellor than a cop. So, how you like working with the Feds, Scotty?'

'No complaints so far . . . but I gotta admit it ain't like the old days. We made one hell of a bad-ass team, didn't we, Sonny?'

'What're you talking about,' said Sonny, 'I carried you the whole way, dude.'

'Oh, oh,' Scotty said, making a face.

Sonny noticed Gina Calabrese – she of the captivating form and fine, fine Italian eyes – signalling to Lou and pointing exaggeratedly at one of the desk extensions. 'Lieutenant? Line twenty-one. He wouldn't give his name.'

Lou snatched up the nearest phone and punched in. 'Rodriguez. Yeah, right, well . . . I know all about that, Leon . . . Mm-hm. Well, I suppose that depends on you.' He snapped his fingers and Crockett tossed him a pen. He jotted down the address Leon gave him. 'Tell you what – you hold tight right there, and I'll call you back in ten minutes and let you know.' He racked off.

'Ooh, cruel, Lou – letting that poor sucker sweat for another ten minutes by some pay phone. You gonna pony up any bet money to cover my prediction?'

'Forget it, Sonny, there's a city ordinance against gambling in the precinct house.' He ripped away the sheet and handed it over. 'Good old Leon is ready to roll. He's all yours.'

'*Gracias*.' He glanced at the sheet. 'Near Dino's Dogs at the beachfront?' At least Leon wasn't crazed enough to try and hide out at his penthouse.

He grabbed his coat and bid everyone *adieu*. He wondered what Tubbs was up to.

Tubbs grabbed a Dino's Dog with all the slop and took a chili-cheese chomp out of the stern end. It wasn't Nathan's, but his stomach had been growling ever since Elvis had swallowed his halibut nearly whole.

Thirty yards away, Leon de Santis did a stationary doubletime dance near a beachfront pay phonebox, obviously waiting without patience for a callback. When the phone did ring, he nearly flew out of his shoes.

Working on a mouthful of hot dog, Tubbs estimated that Crockett had engineered a major scare for the skinny black go-between. Rodriguez had mentioned that Leon had been the guy who arranged the car bomb that shot Eddie Rivera straight up into heaven, so Crockett was probably relishing every second of Leon's torment.

With his dog in one hand and a cold Pepsi in the other, Tubbs settled in to keep an eye on Leon. There was a medium-sized crowd sucking up the sun, sand and surf today, and a volleyball game was in progress between Tubbs' position and Leon's, which provided Tubbs with some visual relief. Some fine specimens of American womanhood were shaking it out there with next to nothing between their flesh and the sun, and Tubbs followed their bobbings and bouncings with interest. The volleyball was embarrassingly bad, but the players were shapely and tasty. Leon was still doing his toe-dance over near the phone. Tubbs' attention dealt diplomatically with his food, all the tanned cleavage and thigh within eyeshot, and Leon. Being a professional, Tubbs spent most of his time watching Leon and regretting what he was missing. A tall woman in a light print dress moved up in line at Dino's. She wore high heels and a flop-brimmed hat. Big sunglasses. She seemed to be here as another spectator, and not a mostly-naked participant. She leaned against the hot dog bar and took in the game for a bit. Then she moved on, walking past Leon and vanishing into a beach house restroom. Leon was trying to keep an eye on everyone on the beach, and not succeeding very well.

A voice came from behind Tubbs as he finished off his dog. 'You're starting to get on my nerves, New York.'

Crockett was a silhouette, looming above Tubbs and blocking out the sun as he squinted up. 'I tailed Leon down here from the courthouse, since I figured he wouldn't bother with jail. How'd you know he was here?'

'It's called protective custody, son; I'll explain it to you sometime. Ever since it *appeared*, in court, that Leon gave us a hand, he's been more than anxious to meet with us and spend a while someplace nice and safe, with lots of locks and no windows, you dig?'

In the distance, Leon was back on the pay phone. A radio pumped out 'Girls Just Want to Have Fun' while the playmates below fumbled through their volleyball game.

'He's probably trying to call Lou back,' said Crockett.

'You got him on pins, all right.'

Leon turned to survey the crowd again, the phone in one hand. Then a red hole blossomed on his white shirt, right at the beltline. His mouth dropped open in pain. Another hole blew away fragments of the shirt in the middle of his ribcage. He jigged backward against the phonebox and a third hole punched out his heart. Then the starch went out of him and he flopped forward, glomming a mouthful of sand, wide-eyed and dead as

70

his disconnected call.

Crockett sprang forward, trying to cleave through the beachgoers, waving his shield. 'Outta the way! Police! Move it!' Tubbs unholstered his pistol and held it up for all to see, which facilitated cutting through the packed people. It didn't matter. Leon was still dead by the time they caught up with him. Quickly they looked around for the shooter. Nothing. Beach scene, mid-day, depressingly normal except for the corpse. Blood puddled on the sand beneath him.

Crockett! Look!' Tubbs had found three neat holes, drilled by the bullets on their way through a pressboard sign next to Dino's.

'Back off, people!' shouted Crockett to the slowly gathering ring of gawkers. The news was spreading back like a flash fire in a tinderbox. Crockett spotted a beach security man. 'You! I want the film outta that woman's camera, and every camera within fifty yards of here. Do it! Now!' The man jumped, not knowing whether to salute.

'He's long gone, Crockett,' said Tubbs. 'Professional hit.'

Crockett moved over to the pay phone to lift the swaying receiver. He stuck in some coins and called Rodriguez.

Disheartened, the duo walked slowly back towards Crockett's parked Corvette. Crockett seemed to be sinking into another self-absorbed funk.

'You know,' said Tubbs, forced and businesslike, 'you and me have been bumpin' knees and elbows ever since we met. I think it's time you reconsidered my offer, pal.'

Crockett couldn't quite believe the line he was being fed. He grunted, dug for his keys, said nothing.

Tubbs filled in the void. 'Yeah, I know – Sonny

Crockett the big maverick, the all-star. Get over yourself, man! You *know* this investigation is dead in the water without me!'

'What the hell are you talking about, New York?'

'Last night's bust,' Tubbs said sharply. 'You may recall it? As far as Calderone knows, I made off with both the cash *and* the party favours when I pinched your cigarette boat. I'm going to be hearing from him.'

Crockett stopped messing with the door lock and stood, stony and silent, regarding Tubbs as he might a wino in the park.

'You *need* me, Crockett!'

He shook his head. 'Jeez, what a hard sell. You are not to be believed.' He opened the door and installed himself in the car, hands gripping the wheel. 'I don't know how this is gonna work out, Mister Tubbs...'

'What?'

'You're not exactly up my alley, style and persona-wise. Heaven knows I'm no box of chocolates...'

'Nothing personal, right?'

Crockett accepted the joke and nodded. 'But all things considered, I think you and I might have to submit to some sort of temporary... uh...' He found himself wincing, as if saying the words hurt his mouth. 'Uh... working relationship.'

'How's that?' said Tubbs, twisting the knife with something like glee. He knew he had Crockett over a barrel.

Crockett snorted. 'Let's go check out Leon's. Hop in.'

Tubbs didn't wait to be asked twice.

The building superintendent lording over Leon's home address was a balding little Jewish man, who, every third sentence or so, would pause to yell something into

72

the next room, which presumably contained his little Jewish wife. Crockett and Tubbs heard a voice answer each time, but they never saw anybody.

'You say you're police officers? *Diana, did you call Mr Hershenson about the parts for the heater?*'

Crockett and Tubbs displayed their shields.

'This is a security building, y'know. I'm not supposed to permit entry to unauthorized personages. *Diana, will ya answer the phone, I'm with people down here!*'

'Answer it yourself, Harvey,' shot back a strident voice. 'I'm in the middle of my soap opera!'

'Shouldn't I be asking to see a search warrant, something like that? *Diana, answer the phone, for God's sake!*'

Crockett smoothly drew a folded batch of official-looking papers from his back pocket and began to read: 'City of Miami, Dade County, Court of Myron T. Bradshaw . . .'

Harvey wearily began to lead Crockett and Tubbs up the stairs. Diana's protests dwindled away behind them.

'. . . hereby granting a warranted inspection of the premises of one Leon Abdullah de Santis this twentieth day of . . .'

'Please, please,' Harvey knuckled under. 'Stop. It sounds like my wife, droning on. Here's the keys. Just drop 'em in the mail slot downstairs when you're done.' Then he turned and headed back downstairs to his room. 'Mr de Santis' is at the end of the hall.' He pointed and was gone. When Crockett closed his hand around the keys, Tubbs grabbed the search warrant, intending to ask how Crockett knew he'd need one in time to put it through channels.

He scrutinised the document. 'Hey, this here's a two-year warranty on a set of steel-belted radials,' he said with a disapproving glance.

'No, really? Gosh.' He bent to key the lock and discovered the door was already open. 'Aw, *man* . . . dammit!' He swung the door back anyway, knowing what he'd see.

The living room looked as though a twister had rearranged it. Sofas were overturned, leather upholstery was knifed apart, drawers hung askew with clothing hanging out, curtains lay pooled on the floor, broken glass sparkled, cushions were gutted and bleeding shredded foam, chairs were rent to pieces, picture frames were shattered and dissected. Calderone's night army had come and gone like commandos, taking with them any hope of new leads . . . and they hadn't had to mess with the super, thought Crockett. How the hell were they supposed to fight *this*?

Tubbs was already methodically combing through the destruction in the living room. His enthusiasm annoyed Crockett, who desultorily turned over a few items, and went through the motions.

'There's always a chance they missed something that means nothing to Calderone, but might help us out,' said Tubbs.

'Slim to none,' said Crockett, deflated by the mess before his eyes. 'In football we call this a fourth down passing situation.'

Tubbs froze, then looked at Crockett with an unexplained new awareness, as though Sonny had just peeled off a face mask to reveal someone Tubbs recognized. 'Crockett, yeah,' said Tubbs. 'James Sonny Crockett, am I right?'

Sounding like a teacher addressing a mildly retarded child, Crockett said, 'Very *good*, Tubbs – next week we'll work on *your* name.'

'No, no, I mean, you used to be some kind of football player . . .'

With a weariness borne of repetition, Crockett said, 'University of Florida. Wide receiver. Number 88. That was a couple of centuries ago.'

Tubbs seemed mildly excited. 'My brother used to *rave* about you, man. One time, you made some kind of winning touchdown at the last minute –'

'Screen pass. Ninety-two yards. Six seconds remaining. Winning TD against Alabama. You gotta get your details right, Tubbs.'

'Man, football bores the *backside* offa me.'

Taken aback, Crockett muttered, 'Figures.' Now he was a little embarrassed.

'Sorry I don't fit the popular black cliché of the rabid sports nut, Sonny. But my brother was crazy about you. I was about fourteen when you were playing college ball. He called you the funk-ay honk-ay.'

Crockett smiled despite himself.

'Not that Vice ain't the most glamorous gig in the world, but what gives, Crockett? You must've had half the scouts in the NFL on your trail.'

Crockett resumed his noncommittal search. 'I traded in my fame and glory for two years in the Southeast Asian conference.'

'Vietnam?'

'Naw, Coney Island,' he said snidely. 'I came back Stateside with a screwed-up right knee, courtesy of a VC 60-millimetre mortar fragment. My time in the forty was six-point-five. Real stellar. That was a one-way ticket to Palookaville.'

'A man's gotta do what a man's gotta do,' Tubbs said, expansively, digging through a scattering of vandalised books, cheap, imitation-leather bound book club editions of the one hundred classics of world literature. *War and Peace. Crime and Punishment. Great Expectations. Uncle Tom's Cabin.* 'Most of these have never even been cracked.' Tubbs examined the spines. Out of the hollowed spine of a fat volume of the collected works of Mark Twain protruded the patterned edge of a thin booklet, like a little black address book. Obviously the library had been rifled, the pages riffled through, and the books dumped on the floor. Impact had caused the edge of the address booklet to scoot forth. Tubbs withdrew it and flipped through the pages. Only one held writing.

'No names,' he said, holding it up for Crockett to see. 'Just numbers.'

'Well, glory be ...' Crockett scanned the list of numerals. 'You win the Sherlockian Award, Tubbs. We can back-trace these numbers through Ma Bell.'

'Leon was *très* panicked back at the courthouse,' said Tubbs as they left the building, after Sonny had dropped the useless door keys. 'But how did Calderone's hitter know where he'd be? I know for a fact the only tail on him was mine ... and he was fighting not to be seen. Took cabs all the way to the beach. Changed five times, had the drivers running lights and taking roundabout routes. I don't know much about the local arteries, Sonny, but I do know it doesn't take an hour and ten minutes to drive in a straight line to the beach.'

'What're you getting at?'

'I'm sayin' the only people who knew where Leon wanted to be picked up were cops. You got a leak in your department the size of the East River.'

Even though Crockett had considered this possibility, it arrested him to hear it vocalized by Tubbs, and the eyes of the two men locked for one grim moment. Then he said, 'I'll worry about *my* department. Unless you got a secretary back at your motel, I suggest *you* worry about getting back there and waiting for Calderone to call.' He had to stop by the squad room and see if ballistics had produced anything scintillating on the bullets that had relieved Leon of his miserable life. He already suspected there would be no good news to hear.

One thing Crockett did not expect to find down at the precinct house was Gina Calabrese.

She was wearing conventional street clothes, not her flashy hooker garb, and almost escaped before he caught up with her in the corridor. She still looked fine enough for him to slap on what remnants of charm were still available to him in his unshaven, drug dealer state. They had both seen each other 'on' and 'off', had bared their souls, in a sense, to each other. For weeks he had been trying to get the message across to Gina that now that his separation from Caroline was official and the divorce hearing was being scheduled, it was okay for them to proceed with their own budding relationship. Gina seemed to want to know him better, but for reasons unknown – *yet* unknown, he corrected – she was holding back. But he knew she admired the way he kept trying.

He slithered around her and blocked the corridor. Smiling, he began: 'Gina, darlin', I got a small favour to ask of you.'

Her brown eyes sparkled with bemusement. 'Is this one of those infamous Sonny Crockett favours that grows into three favours by the time you stop talking? Or do you mean a "small" favour in the way that babysitting a crocodile with an upset tummy for a *whole afternoon* was small?'

He gave her a what-can-I-say shrug. 'Alligator. Repeat after me – *alli*-gator.' She stood waiting. 'I got some rolls of *turista* film from the beach I need developed in a hurry.'

She sighed. 'Sonny, I gotta be in costume and on the pavement in less than an hour . . .'

'So you'll have to go right by the lab, right? You could drop the stuff off for me.'

Knowing she'd waste more time arguing, she simply held out her hand. Crockett gave her the rolls of film and she stowed them in her shoulder bag.

'As a token of my appreciation, how about dinner tonight. Now I *know* you're not working tonight.' His happy tone suggested it might be good for both of them.

'I'll think about it.'

Her reply nearly caused him to whoop, rejoicing... but he slid in another favour instead. Fortunes of the job. 'By the by, I also need a computer bio on a New York narc by the name of Raphael Tubbs.'

'That new guy?'

'Yep – as long as you're downtown.' He handed over a slip of paper with Tubbs' name written on it.

Gina looked to the heavens for relief. 'Jeez, give him an inch and he thinks he's a ruler!'

He touched her cheek, then nearly lost himself. 'See you tonight.'

'You wish,' she said, and strode off down the hall just as Crockett's extension started ringing. He dallied for one ring just to watch Gina's switching hips, then grabbed the phone.

'We're back in business, my man,' came Tubbs' voice.

'What's the scoop?' Gina was out the door.

'Calderone's right hand just called about the cash. Name's uh ... Trini de Soto?'

'A voice a little on the festive side? A cross between Tito Puente and Carol Channing?'

'*Joo god it, mang.*'

'I'll pick you up at the motel in fifteen minutes.' He racked the receiver and dashed out. It was getting to be a busy two days.

## 7

Fat Sal's stank up Little Havana in two directions from
its address, with the mustard-gas odour of grease-
griddle Mexican fare – beans, bulk jack cheese, fried
tortillas and *carne asada*, Dos Equis in bottles and
Tecate in cans. The interior was pure south-of-the-
border phony baloney, with artificial adobe and
sombreros and serapes stapled to the walls. The smoke
from Cuban hand-rolled cigars fouled the air, and the
bar was fully stocked with a shoulder-to-shoulder row
of loud hustlers filling up on barbequed appetizers and
downing neat shots of rum with beer chasers.
Occasionally they drowned out the freight-train *salsa*
chugging forth from the jukebox in the corner by
whooping it up over a televised soccer game, which was
radiating downwards in bizarre, sputtering colours
from a badly-tuned TV bolted above the bar. The play-
by-play was in incomprehensible machine-gun Spanish.
It appeared to Crockett that Tubbs could follow the
lingo.

Not that it mattered, because Trini de Soto's clothing
was so loud it could overwhelm Fat Sal's usual customer
commotion, even when Trini was keeping his mouth
shut, which he wasn't. Vigorously . . .

'Joo see, most of that Merielito riff-raff stuck in
detention with me'd kill the time watching *Family Feud*,
mang,' de Soto philosophized around a mouthful of

green chile enchilada, dead serious. "*Hollywood Squares.
In Searcha de Ryan's Hope* – all that gar-bahge, eh? Not
me, mang! I figure – "Dig it, Trini, joo could be stuck in
this dump *six months*, mang, waiting for jour papers!
Use the time, mang – improve jour *mind*!"'

Tubbs knocked back a slug of iced coffee while
Crockett tossed an annoyed glance towards the soccer
match on the tube. 'You read a lot of books, then, huh?'

Trini squinted in disappointment, forking more food.
'Joo missing *my* point, mang! I skip alla that network
jive. I tune into the old classics – *I Love Lucy, Father He
Know Best, Leave it to Joo Beaver* ... *Gilligan's Island*.
S'where I learn to speak English so good, mang. The
Golden Age of TV.' He waved his fork around to make
his point, lowering his voice confidentially. 'And forget
about dat Desi Arnaz, mang. The fact that dat dude
never copped an Academy Award says something very
deep about the American psyche.' Trini was very much
like a parody of an androgynous Latino pimp from a bad
foreign horror movie.

'See?' said Tubbs. 'Who says TV doesn't educate the
public.' That brought Crockett's attention back.

'Those New York critics sabotaged poor Desi,' said
Crockett, more to Tubbs. 'Don't let it throw you, Trini.'
He plugged down a cold draft of San Miguel Dark.

Trini mopped his face and dumped his napkin atop
his oval plate. 'Anyhow, I bore joo enough with my
fascinating background, mang. Joo got the money?' He
had switched to business without a blink of warning, his
eyes betraying a killer coldness lurking beneath the
Speedy Gonzales exterior.

Tubbs was ready for him, meeting his sudden hard
gaze evenly. 'Not till I see Calderone,' he said, shaking
his head.

Trini became even more expansive, cuffing Tubbs on

the biceps. 'But *Teddy*, I'm his personal representative!'

Tubbs made his Teddy Prentiss into a no-bull negotiator. 'Look – I didn't have to show here today. This is strictly gratis. After that little fiasco on the docks, I'm through dealing with the middleman! You tell Calderone he wants his cash, he deals with me, Teddy Prentiss, personally – no more intermediaries.'

De Soto drew a semi-exasperated breath sharply through his nostrils. 'That is difficult to arrange, my good friend.'

'Tell him to think of it as a contingency bonus on the next load,' Tubbs prodded. 'That nickel-bag stash you sent me the other night won't even cover my bar tab on the airplane.'

That got Trini's attention. He chewed on it for a thoughtful moment. 'And what would, Señor Prentiss . . ?'

Crockett leaned in with a knowing smile. 'Sky's the limit, *amigo*.'

Trini shifted his sights, keeping up his slaphappy persona. 'And joo, Mr Burnett – what's jour stake in all this?'

Tubbs picked it up, making sure Trini divided his attention. 'Burnett will handle all my transportation.'

'A wise choice, Teddy,' nodded Trini approvingly. To Crockett, he added, 'Jour reputation as a . . . boating enthusiast, precedes joo, my friend.'

'If you mean via that slack-jawed Leon,' Crockett said, 'Word I got was he's done preceded *all* of us.'

De Soto burst into a hearty laugh. 'That's *muy bien*, hm?' He stood up. The meeting was done. 'Nine o'clock, Key Biscayne Club, hokay? Then you bring the money.'

'Nine o'clock,' said Crockett. They both watched de Soto saunter out, giving an elegant wave in passing to several other regulars. When Crockett turned back to Tubbs, the black cop was making a face.

'Ah yes, Trini,' said Crockett, catching on. 'That dude gives new meaning to the word "alien". C'mon, let's blow this pop stand.'

'Didn't know you hulking football types were into soccer,' Tubbs said, indicating the TV they'd left behind.

'I'm not. I hate it. It's just that there's a Dolphins game on Channel Four.'

'Not in Little Havana, there ain't.'

Crockett sulked all the way out to his car. 'That pea-brained Jimmy Carter signs out a blank cheque to one hundred and twenty-five *thousand* of these boat-lifted *frijole*-pluckers, a good twenty-five percent of whom are known felons, and five years later Castro's still laughing his butt off while us native sons can't even check up on a red-blooded American football game...'

'How much money you got on it?'

Crockett squashed his face in an expression of comic annoyance. 'I'm trying to make a serious socio-political point here, Tubbs – what the hell does that have to do with whether or not I can –'

'How much?'

Deflated and sour, Crockett said, 'A hundred bucks.'

'Capitalism strikes again.'

'Big deal.' Together they climbed into the Corvette. After a few miles blew beneath them in silence, Tubbs said, 'I don't know whether my sense of humour can stand another meal with Trini de Soto so soon.' His stomach was churning out acid on behalf of the fact that he might be in the same room as Francisco Calderone in a little over six hours.

'I haven't told you the best part yet,' grinned Sonny. 'As part of our cover we get Gina and Trudy tonight.'

Tubbs stared at his stubbly partner, eyebrows up, as though he'd just gotten a birthday gift. 'Trudy's fine,' he said after a moment. 'I like that idea... you need a date, you just ring up Vice and they send over some good looking personages of the opposing gender, yessss...' Posing as a dope dealer had its little perks. You had to dress and eat first class, absolutely... unless you had established an identity as eccentric as Sonny's cover. Sonny's hallmarks were his expensive speedboat and his casual disdain for expensive clothing and cars. He had the boats, the cars, the clothes, but he made sure the pushers and runners with whom he dealt saw that he didn't care about them. Tubbs preferred to cut a more classy cover image, covering his lithe frame with tailored threads and flawlessly speaking the native dialects.

As they hit the Venetian Causeway, Tubbs said, 'I've been doing a little thinking about possibles on your departmental leak.'

'Yeah? What're you getting at?'

'Well... how well do you know this Lieutenant Rodriguez of yours? He's really the point man in the whole operation.'

Crockett's eyes glared like fanned coals. 'You're just down here on a courtesy pass, New York, so you'd better take a major conversational detour right now!'

Sometimes Sonny seemed to be on his side, unreservedly, Tubbs thought. Then he'd turn like a wolf puppy or a striking cottonmouth. 'Hey, lighten up, man, I was just asking –'

Crockett jumped in with another of his infamous shout-down interruptions: 'You're just *asking* about a man I consider to be one of the most righteous cops in the entire country, who I've worked with for damned near six years, which is five years, eleven months, and twenty-nine days longer than I've known *you*, my friend!'

With equal force, Tubbs shot back, 'Yeah, well since you know him so well, maybe you can explain an eighteen *thousand* dollar deposit he made at Miami Federal ten days ago . . . ?'

Crockett didn't know whether to be surprised first, or enraged. He stomped on the gas to cover the fact that Tubbs' news had blind-sided him. 'You're doing makes on my friends?!'

'Just a little local research – it's called stayin' *alive*, son.' He mimicked Crockett's tone from the earlier incident on the beach. 'I'll explain it to you sometime. How about that Switek and Zito, for example? Zito looks like his bulb lost half its wattage a year ago, and Switek don't win no loving cups for covert surveillance, neither. It ever occur to you they blew the bust with Leon on purpose? And how about the Feds on the case? How about this guy Scotty Wheeler?'

'Whoa,' said Crockett, firm now, his tolerance gone. 'That's where I draw the line. You stop or you walk, New York.'

'Just wanted to occupy your mind, *mon*. Think on it.'

Crockett barely gave Tubbs another syllable until they split up and rendezvoused for the dinner engagement. He was not about to let Tubbs know he hadn't heard about Rodriquez' enormous deposit.

Gina and Trudy were better than fine; they were *bad*, and that was *good*.

The Key Biscayne Club was another in a long string of high-priced meat racks, a private disco-dinner house catering to deposed Central American fast-laners, mostly Columbian coke royalty. Armani-tailored Marielito hitmen, and assorted cash-flashing aerobicized bimbos. Gina Calabrese was inside – almost – of a cowl-necked affair that wound down towards a tight skirt that flashed a lot of perfect thigh; Trudy Joplin was similarly bejewelled and begowned. Crockett had begrudingly abandoned the table to trade fatuous nods with a dude who had recognized him – as Burnett, of course – Twenty-Four Hour Martinizing Marty Goins, who ran a money-laundering operation out of the Cayman Islands. As soon as Crockett had left the table, Tubbs had turned the conversation to the most obvious tasty topic.

'He told you he *volunteered* for Vietnam?' said Gina, with an incredulous little-girl dip of her head, her dark, beguiling eyes flashing with laughter. 'Aside from an occasional message parlour raid, Sonny Crockett never raised his hand for anything in his life.'

Trudy had her hand on Tubbs' arm, and that was just fine with Tubbs. 'He probably told you he earned that bad kneecap of his in combat, right?'

Tubbs savoured an after-dinner snifter of Martell. 'Uh – kind of.'

Gina and Trudy swapped knowing looks. Gina sipped her vodka and said, 'Story *I* heard was that he got totally *blitzed* in the wake of some big-deal touchdown his last year on the U of F team and fell two storeys trying to climb out of some baton-twirler's dormitory window at five in the morning.'

Trudy said, 'You call *that* combat, honey, he couldn't walk for all the Purple Hearts.'

They all cracked up. Tubb liked them both; the game they were all playing was the upside of Vice duty – a first class meal in an exclusive club, drinks and finery, laughs and friends in the midst of the pit of evil. It would be great if they could all just retire to Crockett's sloop and ignore the harsh reasons *why* they were running this elaborate cover in the first place.

One of Sonny's big hands appeared on either of the women's shoulders, and he leaned in. Tubbs was amazed that Crockett hadn't shaved, even for this dinner. He seemed to have a permanent three-day growth of beard on his face that never got longer or shorter. 'Enjoying the wit and wisdom of Mr Prentiss, ladies?'

He barely had time to sit and address an untouched bourbon and branch water when Trini de Soto made his typical showstopping entrance, gliding through the crush of dancers and drinkers in a broad-shouldered Claude Montana ensemble that made him look like a refugee from a roadshow of *Zoot Suit*. His pupils were no bigger than pinpricks; he was obviously coked to the gills and in a festive mood.

'Sorry to keep joo waiting so long.' He extended a hand limply towards Sonny. 'Señor Burnett. I trust dinner was to jour satisfaction?'

Crockett and Tubbs had stood; they all settled for Hollywood handshakes while Tubbs, acting a trifle stoned himself, gushed, '*Righteous*, mon!'

Ultrasuave, Trini bowed to the ladies. Gina stood and proffered her hand, which he grasped long enough to plant a dry Continental kiss. His glazed gaze bounced from her legs to her chest to her eyes. '*Los ojos son precioses.*' Trudy got the same treatment. Tubbs felt a pang of something like envy; were the girls actually impressed by this jerk, or were they merely terrific actresses?

Gina and Trudy recognized their cue, as business was about to be discussed. 'Well,' Gina said demurely. 'If you boys will excuse us, Trudy and I are due for a little paint and body work.' She winked at de Soto, who watched their bodies work as they strolled off for the

86

ladies room.

'*Muy hermosas, eh?*'

Tubbs attracted Trini's notice by producing a coat-check ticket and handing it over. 'It's in the cloakroom, mon,' he said, low. 'A hundred and twenty even. Good faith money for a working relationship.' He grinned agreeably. De Soto handed the ticket off to a young Latino who drifted discreetly past the table. He hadn't even been signalled. They were being watched every second, Tubbs thought.

De Soto leaned back, sucking the air as though it were laced with primo Thai stick. Indicating the room with a theatrically expensive gesture, he started in. 'I *love* this place, mang. Pretty people, first-class restrooms, selective door policy.' Catching the dance tune, he mouthed along. 'Honnly in Miami ... is Cooba so ... farrr awayyyyyy ... !' Then he broke apart in a fluting, unhinged giggle.

'Earth to Trini ... ?' said Crockett.

'Don't mind me, mang, I've been up there for four days running, y'know?'

'I've had days like that,' Crockett nodded.

Trini got a hold of himself. 'What kind of weight are we talking about here, Teddy?'

Teddy/Tubbs considered this under another sip. 'I can have up to ten million in US bills at my disposal by noon tomorrow. Forty grand a kilo, tops – you figure it out.' He was all smiles.

Trini tasted this information and found it intriguing. 'I'm not making any promises, of course ... but joo may have come into the picture at a very opportunistic time. Tell me about this killer boat of jours, Burnett.'

'Thirty-nine feet, all engine, can handle a good eighty kilos and still outrun any chase boat the Coast Guard's got.'

'In that case, joo might want to have a second one just like it on call.' Trini was getting happier and higher the more he heard.

My god! Tubbs thought. They were sitting here nursing overpriced joy juice and talking a probable load of something between a hundred and sixty to two hundred and fifty kilos! You could build a house just with the bricks . . .

'*Todo está bien*,' said Trini, hands on the table. 'If joo hear from us at all, it'll be sometime tomorrow.'

Crockett was smooth. 'We'll be at the boat number, day or night.'

Trini rose and was apparently about to forget them in his heightened state of chemical awareness. Tubbs tapped his forearm. 'Not so fast, Trini, *mon* . . . you said that Calderone would be here.'

Crockett shot a glance at Tubbs, as if to say, *what difference*? but Trini turned back and nodded with a glint in his heavy-lidded, drug-fogged eyes. 'He *has* been here, mang . . .'

A waiter stood before them bearing an iced magnum of vintage 1976 Veuve Clicquot Champagne La Grande Dame – a hundred-dollar bottle of bubbly. 'Compliments of the gentleman across the room, sirs,' he said, extending the tray for inspection.

Tubbs looked in the direction indicated. His heart thudded hard when he saw Calderone sitting in a lavish three-quarter booth, a nineteen-year-old Quaaludette on either side and one of his hulking bodyguards standing nearby, bearing the briefcase retrieved from the cloakroom. The goons were not the ones Tubbs had wasted in the Bronx. The pocky-faced, silver-and-crude-oil haired drug magnate raised his champagne glass to toast Tubbs and Crockett long-distance. De Soto had melted into the throng. Tubbs kept staring.

The control-boothed DJ spun 'All Night Long'.

'Hey, Tubbs –' Crockett began, but Tubbs shrugged him off and started moving across the dance floor, beelining for Calderone.

Sonny had no idea what Tubbs might do, taking the initiative this way. If he chased after him it would look bad. So he grabbed his seat and wrapped his hand around his bourbon, watching, scared that some unknown pressure valve had abruptly burst in Tubbs' mind.

*Well my friends the time has come / To raise the roof and have some fun / Go away the work to be done / And let the music play on / Everybody sing, everybody dance / And lose yourself in wild romance / We going to party, come on and fiesta forever . . . Come on and sing along . . .*

Tubbs' heart was going like a volcano, but he kept his veneer of cool intractably on, and glided towards Calderone sleek as a silken cat. The bodyguard made way for him. And Calderone, the little man with so much power, regarded him from the raised, throne-like vantage of the booth. His expression was open and curious, yet superior and condescending.

*'All night long . . . all night . . .'*

Tubbs smiled. 'Hospitable gesture, Mr Calderone. I thank you.'

Calderone extended his hand. His shake was very different from Trini de Soto's sexually ambiguous wringing.

'Teddy Prentiss,' Tubbs continued. 'I'm looking forward to doing business with you.' He ached to tear out a gun and blow Calderone apart, to put a slug in his skull and watch his brains decorate the chintz behind the booth. The dope-dazed teenyboppers snuggling up to him weren't even aware of what planet they were on. The bodyguard was no threat to Tubbs. He could smash a highball glass and spoon out Calderone's eyes, he could drive his thumbs into his throat and crush his larynx. A hard chop to the windpipe; brain death. He felt capable of sawing the Columbian's heart out with one of the steak knives on the table. Calderone died in agony a thousand times in the space of their polite social handshake.

But neither Tubbs nor Crockett had come packed. To tote guns into this place would have been a big mistake if any of Calderone's minions had decided to pat them down. Instead of killing the man instantly, Tubbs released his hand. The touch of Calderone's dry, powdered and perfumed flesh made his stomach roll.

'Welcome to Miami, Señor Prentiss.'

Back at the table, Crockett gulped hard, but all seemed well as Tubbs and Calderone shook hands and exchanged a few meaningless words. Then Tubbs turned briskly and headed back. Gina and Trudy returned first, sharing some private joke, then clueing Crockett in.

'Regular Hoover convention in the loo tonight,' Gina shook her head. 'Six legs to a stall.'

'That's why they call it the powder room, dear,' smiled Trudy.

Crockett registered all this, but was vitally concerned for Tubbs. 'Hey, partner – ?'

Tubbs sat, said nothing, stared straight ahead at some memory none of them could see.

'You okay?'

Teddy Prentiss returned. 'Yeah, mon. Everything's first-rate. No problem.'

Crockett hefted Calderone's uncorked offering. 'Champagne, anybody?' he said, pouring a glass for himself first.

Trudy didn't sit down. 'Look, I don't know about you

90

party types, but *I* gotta be at work tomorrow. You remember work? Yeah. So... can I drop anybody?'

Tubbs' face lit up. He seemed to have recovered now. 'Yeah,' he said, grandly offering himself. He stood up and took Trudy's arm.

Gina looked at them and said to Trudy, 'I'll talk to you tomorrow.' Everybody swapped goodnights and Tubbs and Trudy moved off.

'I think Tubbs is in love,' grinned Crockett.

'I thought his name really was Prentiss,' Gina said, a puzzled expression darkening her face.

'Naw. Raphael Tubbs. That's why I asked you to run the computer check. Didn't come back with anything, did you?'

'Sure as hell did,' said Gina. 'Listen, Sonny, I don't know who that joker is for real, but the readout told me that Detective Raphael Tubbs has been dead and buried for over three weeks now.'

Crockett's glass fell to the floor and rolled. Fortunately it was empty. But that didn't change the look of shock on his face.

## 8

Tubbs' hotel line buzzed twelve, thirteen times as Crockett paced the deck of the sloop. On each return trip towards the galley hatch he was stared down by a dour, sleepy-eyed Elvis, who found this whole human business of trust and betrayal irrelevant. His 'gator eyes glowed in the darkness like yellow cigarette ends.

'Come on, come on, pick it up – !' Crockett goaded the impassive phone. 'I should've *known* it was some kind of setup! Guy drops in outta nowhere, sketchy background, third-hand referral ... Jesus, I above all people should know a flimsy cover story when it begins to stink ...'

He punched the disconnect on the remote phone set, and angrily put the number through one more time.

Gina relaxed in a deck chair, high heels tipped over on the deck of the *St Vitus Dance*, putting away a slow drink at leisure and trying to select a cassette from Crockett's eclectic music library. With a shake of her head she compromised on a Jimmy Buffett album, slotted it into the tape machine and watched as the opening strains of 'One Particular Harbor' made the LED meters jump in the dark. Elvis, she saw, was cosied up on top of his blue security blanket.

Crockett rambled on as the phone rang unanswered. 'Cardinal rule in this damned business; never trust *anybody*! Who knows who this guy really is, who he could be working for! DEA, State, County, customs, the CIA or the Special Assignments branch of the MIRG... hell, for all I know, he's another one of Calderone's ringers, with a cock and bull story two miles wide, just looking for a sucker narc like me to con...'

Gina, the voice of reason, overrode him. 'Sonny, there's not a hell of a lot you can do right now anyway... unless you want to camp outside his hotel all night. You *could* get a grip on yourself.'

Riled, he was about to snap something when he saw the good humour and concern in her eyes. He hung up the phone, gave Elvis a perfunctory pat on the snout, dumped some half-melted icecubes and Wild Turkey into a fresh glass, and leaned against the starboard rail, near Gina. His anger evaporated. 'I don't know...' He shook his head like a confused puppy. 'Maybe I'm getting too old for this line of work. Scraping by on four hours sleep a day... living undercover for weeks at a time... Dealer this week, outlaw biker the next, smut peddler the next. If it's Tuesday, I must be working drugs.' She smiled, so he gave it another inch. 'It's hell on the old nervous system. Disastrous on a marriage...'

'Nothing's tougher on a relationship than the kind of work we do,' said Gina. After a contemplative silence she added, 'Do you ever forget who you are?'

'Forget?' He gave her a sad laugh. 'Darlin', sometimes I *remember* who I am. But what the heck, right? I've got a terrifc six-year-old boy... jeez, six years old.' He didn't want the silence to become too awkward, so he continued with his list. 'I've got pick of the litter on overpriced confiscated automobiles, not one boat, but two, a really swell freaked-out alligator... and a recently announced free agency in the Southeast String Bikini League. Like the song says, "She left me at Sears... and I cried all the way to Walgreens."' He toasted Elvis (who grunted), then Gina, then Bal Harbor in general, then drank.

'You're such a fraud, Sonny Crockett.'

'What?' He was all mock innocence.

'You can play that beach-bum cowboy routine with the football lingo and the beer commercial mentality from now till Doomsday, but I'll never swallow it.'

He wasn't meeting her eyes. 'Whoops, trapped again.'

'You're just as scared and screwed up as anyone.'

'You know something Gina?' He smiled winningly. 'You can be a real pain in the butt sometimes . . . but I like you.' In this at least, he was sincere. It was a gap in his emotional shield he was permitting her to see. 'I like you a lot.'

'I like you too, Sonny.' Simple, direct.

'Oh, really?' He saw his chance to shift the topic from himself. 'So why've you tossed back four dinner invitations in three weeks? You wouldn't have come along tonight if you hadn't had Trudy there to block tackle.'

She was going to suggest that Trudy had taken Tubbs back to her apartment, just to keep from addressing the touchy business with Sonny, but decided against it. That was too fast, even for New York speed. Instead, she said, 'My father was of venerable old Roman stock. He always told me never to get involved with a man on the rebound. Look at you, Sonny – you're bouncing so hard you're nearly off the court.'

He tried to steer around what at first seemed to him no more than a female weirdness from left field. 'What the hell's *that* mean?'

'You're still in love with Caroline.' There was regret in her voice.

*Thump*. Her words went straight to his heart, and not

knowing whether he was guilty or not terrified him. He tried to cover it up with swagger. 'Try again, lady...'

Their hands had found each other during this impromptu psychoanalysis, and now Gina pulled hers away. 'I should go,' she submitted quietly. She stood, kissed him lightly, as if in understanding, then went below, presumably to collect her shoulder bag and freshen up.

Sonny stood alone on the deck, feeling a little sorry for himself. What could send Gina away, he thought, after she'd come all the way out to the marina with him in the wee hours of the morning, if not a failure of his charm? He did not even have *that* left, apparently.

The lights went out belowdecks. Crockett turned and saw Elvis staring down, reproachfully. 'What're *you* lookin' at?' he said, and the alligator rolled languorously over on his blanket. When Gina didn't appear immediately, Sonny stuck his head into the hatchway. 'Gina? You okay?'

'Yeah,' came her voice from the dark doorway. 'Give me your hand.'

Crockett did, and found himself yanked down the steps and into Gina's embrace. His arms went around her and he caressed the smooth, bare skin of her shoulders and back.

Elvis, realizing he was going to have spend the night by himself out in the open, grunted like a lonely hound dog and plopped his muzzle down on his blanket.

Crockett slept soundly, more comfortably than he had in weeks. Having another warm body in one's bed did great things for one's world outlook. The ocean smelled like daylight but he was not yet ready to rise; he wanted to relish this experience, slow time down if necessary.

Eyes shut in a dreamy semi-doze, he rolled over in the

cabin's queen-sized bed and draped an arm over Gina. He instantly registered something wrong. Gina did not have armoured scales and fish breath.

He opened his eyes. Elvis, bunked in the vacancy left by Gina, pretended to be asleep, a self-satisfied smirk on his prow.

The growling digital clock mercilessly proclaimed eight o'clock in the morning. Without much hope, Crockett sat up. 'Gina?' Her stuff was gone. Elvis' blue blanket was on the stairs. She'd left the hatch open and the 'gator had crawled in to occupy what he thought to be his rightful place.

'Terrific,' he muttered. The last thing he'd figured Gina for was a fast exit. Then he heard footsteps on the dock. 'Gina ... ?'

Outside, Tubbs overheard him. 'Hey, Crockett, you decent?' he said, a little loudly, to penetrate the closed shutters on the sloop. 'Rise and shine, buddy boy!' No response. 'Hey, Crockett – if that stoned-out reptile is hangin' around where I can't see him, you tell him to cool or I'll make a suitcase outta him ... Crockett?'

He bent to pick up Elvis' security blanket from the galley steps. Elvis noted this trangression from his fat sprawl on the bed, and made a bull-throated tremor of warning. 'Hey, Elvis, you sure are lookin' ... uh, scaly this morning.' He was beginning to feel a little more at ease around the dinosauric creature. 'You got any idea in that acid-bath brain of yours where Crockett might be at?' He'd noticed the mostly-empty fifth of Wild Turkey up on deck.

In response to his question, a large hand slammed into his throat, lifting his feet from the floor and bulldogging him into the opposite wall. An impossibly wide gun barrel was shoved into his gut, and when Tubbs opened his eyes he saw Sonny Crockett, sweating, paranoiac, and ready to off him in an instant.

'This here's a flare gun, sucker,' snarled Crockett. 'It fires an incendiary cartridge as big as a can of deodorant. Now unless you want your entire intestinal tract to light up like Cape Canaveral, you've got exactly ten seconds to tell me who the hell you are!'

Tubbs drifted into shock. This couldn't be a joke. 'You *crazy*, Sonny, what the – ?'

'Eight seconds!' Sonny was not kidding.

'You know who I am, man!'

Louder, Crockett shouted right in Tubbs' face. 'Raphael Tubbs bought the farm six weeks ago in that New York shootout with Calderone! *Four seconds*! Who are you, man?' The flare gun jammed harder against Tubbs' ribcage.

Tubbs saw the light. 'His brother.'

Elvis had plopped down and scuttled over from the bed, and waited with his mouth hinged open for a drumstick, in case Tubbs was lying. Crockett held fast.

'I'm his *brother*, Crockett!' Now Tubbs was fuming. 'I know we all look alike to you Southern crackers but we're not the Bobbsey Twins, man. Look at the picture! *Look* at it!'

Crockett backed off, disoriented, and grabbed the blow-up of Calderone with the New York contacts off his desk top.

Blowing off an adrenalin high as Crockett calmed, Tubbs said, 'Raphael was the *best* – he was the reason I became a cop.'

Crockett peered doubtfully at the blow-up, then at Tubbs, then back. 'The older brother? The one who liked football?'

Tubbs nodded. 'My ID's in my right pocket.'

The gun was still aimed, but the threat had gone out of it. Crockett fished the wallet from Tubbs' tailored jacket. His jaw hung open when he examined the identity card. 'Tubbs Ricardo,' he read. 'Sixty-First Precinct, the Bronx . . . Armed Robbery Division . . .?' With a hiss of disgust, he added, 'Don't tell me. Your friends call you "Rico", right?' His attention locked on something else on the card. 'Only *four years* out of the Academy?'

The gun gradually lowered, till it was pointed at the floor. Elvis moved out of the line of fire as gracefully as an overweight, ten-foot alligator with an LSD hangover could.

'Homicide up north was batting zero,' said Tubbs.

'Why?' Crockett said wonderingly. 'The "inter-departmental memo" Lou mentioned? The priority clearance? All forged?'

'You're not stupid, Sonny – how the hell *else* could I have gotten down here so soon after Calderone blew New York? A Bronx street cop on a Brooklyn narcotics investigation? What was I supposed to do – tell them there was a death in the family?' His frustration had been backed and bottled up for too long, he was relieved to spill some of it for Sonny, even if Sonny wound up hating him. 'A veteran Detective First Class on assignment doesn't get asked so many stupid questions. That bastard Calderone killed Raphael!'

Crockett was matching him mad for mad. 'Where'd the hundred and twenty grand come from? You print it up in your basement? Or moonlighting, doing your detective impersonation in supper clubs?'

'Brooklyn counterfeiting bust, last August. A New York Vice guy, friend of my brother's, snuck it out of the property room for me.'

'Grand.' He was pacing again. 'Counterfeit setup cash. Fake memos. Forged security clearances. *God* – !' He heaved the flare gun across the cabin as hard as he could. It cleaned off a bookshelf when it shattered. Elvis panicked and slithered under the bed, dragging his blanket with him to protect it from Crockett, who was raving. 'The biggest score of my entire godforsaken career, and I'm teamed up with a black Charles Bronson outlaw on a bloody assassination run!'

'It's called justice, Crockett!' Tubbs protested.

Crockett stabbed a finger towards him. 'It's called *vengeance*, my friend, plain and simple! Now I may seem somewhat unorthodox to the untrained eye, but when it comes to police work I'm strictly business, and I'll be *damned* if I'm gonna put my hide on the firing line for some renegade, hot-headed street cop on a personal vendetta! 'Cause when it gets personal it gets messy, and when it gets messy, the *wrong* people get killed! *Comprende?*'

Tubbs had half-expected an outburst like this. Three Musketeers camaraderie was strictly for Saturday matinees. Crockett stood steaming for a moment, then reached for the phone.

'I'm blowing the whistle on you to Rodriguez. You're outta this operation, Tubbs, as of right now!'

Tubbs slammed his hand down on top of Sonny's, disconnecting the phone. 'There *is* no operation without me, Crockett, remember? Calderone'll back out so fast the vacuum'll suck the air out of your lungs!'

While both their hands were slapjacking it on top of the phone, it started ringing.

'That's them,' said Tubbs. 'Calling for Teddy Prentiss.' Crockett would not remove his hand. He was mad as hell. 'Four people blown away,' pressed Tubbs. 'My brother, dead. Your partner Eddie – *dead*! For nothing? Crockett, please!'

Crockett made a strangling, gutteral sound, then punched the cabin panelling so hard it rocked the boat.

It had to be done. 'Answer it!'

Tubbs' manner changed with the speed of flipping channels on a TV set. He snatched up the receiver. 'Yeah, mon?'

Trini de Soto had good news for Teddy Prentiss.

The dark slash of Rodriguez' eyebrow elevated in interest. 'Three *hundred* pounds of coke? Whew.' He tried to smile, but the cigar permanently rooted in his face made it a kind of gallows grimace.

Crockett was proud of the potential bust, but Tubbs had planted in him the nagging kernel of doubt. Who in the department was the info leak, and why was Lou so happy about the deal with Calderone? 'Eight o'clock tonight,' he affirmed. 'Panamanian-registered shrimp boat off Virginia Key.'

'Terrific.'

Crockett shuffled through the stack of tourist photo blow-ups he'd gleaned from the beach murder scene of Leon de Santis. Tubbs was visible in one shot. Mostly the pictures were standard tourist junk, focusing either on the ocean or on the volleyball lovelies. Dino's Dogs was visible at the corner of a few snaps. Regarding the Calderone pickup for that evening, Crockett said, 'I took the liberty of calling a little pre-game strategy in about ten minutes for all the backup men for tonight – Switek and Zito, Hoban and Dibble, Gorman and Augustine. Figured we could all chew on the fine points then.'

'Fine. How about Tubbs?'

Crockett had kept mum about Tubbs' true identity, trusting the young cop almost against his will. 'I got him low-profiling it on the *St Vitus Dance* till the party starts – also in case Trini de Soto calls back on behalf of Calderone.'

'Seems like you two make a pretty fair team after all.'

*You shoulda seen how we started the day*, he thought. But if Tubbs' back-story was true, he'd certainly handled himself professionally during his face-to-face with Calderone at the Key Biscayne Club. Calderone had bought the Teddy Prentiss rap, and Calderone was a killer who wasn't easy to snow. Now Crockett and Rodriguez were sitting around, basking in their egos, secure in the foreknowledge of the stake they were preparing to drive through the heart of the man that two weeks ago Crockett had known only as The Columbian. Tubbs had been responsible.

Through Rodriguez' office window Crockett spotted Gina breezing through the squad room. He moved for the door and was blocked when a desk sergeant stuck her head inside.

'Call for you, Lieutenant,' she said to Rodriguez. 'A Sister Agnes at Immaculate Heart, on line two.'

Crockett stopped, turned back to catch the reaction on Lou's face. Lou looked up from the junkyard of paperwork on his habitually cluttered desk and grinned. 'I'll have to call her back, Trina.' To Crockett he added, 'I'm sending my boy Hector there next fall. Been kind of waiting for them to get back to me, so I figure I'll make *them* wait a few minutes, you know?'

'Good school,' Crockett nodded. 'Wish I could afford to send Billy there.'

Lou sensed Crockett's probing tone and put down the papers. 'What's that supposed to mean?'

*Why are you suddenly defensive, Lou?* Crockett used the same argument he'd used on Eddie Rivera. 'Nothing. Just seems like an awful tough ante to make on a lieutenant's salary...'

Lou stood up then, pushing his glasses down to the bulb of his nose in order to scrutinize Crockett. 'What the hell's wrong with you, Crockett? You wanna know where I got the money – just ask me.'

Immediately, tonelessly, Crockett said, 'Where'd you get the money, Lou?'

'None of your business, detective,' Lou growled. 'Now get your butt out of my office.'

Crockett neatened the stack of photo blow-ups, and took them with him, deciding to check up on Leon's little black address book. He moved to George Maroni's desk. 'Anything yet on the name trace for that list of numbers, George?'

George looked up from his corned beef on rye. 'Almost.'

'I got a briefing to do in a bit. Think you'll have 'em an hour from now?'

'Well, if I don't stop for dessert...'

'I'll buy you a whole Sara Lee cherry cheesecake, George, if you can have 'em then, plus do some blow-ups on these for me, quick – high priority rush.' He dealt the tourist snaps out onto the desk. 'Here. Here and here. My eyes only, pal. Okay?'

There was an urgency in his tone that made George lower his voice confidentially. 'Sure thing, Sonny.'

Crockett looked up and caught Gina watching him from the other side of the squad room. As he noticed her, she reddened and turned away, frittering near the coffee machine. Before Crockett could investigate what *this* behaviour was supposed to mean, Tommy Ray Zito was in his face.

Zito waggled his eyebrows at Gina's hooker get-up and wiped his nose with the back of his hand. 'Boys are in the roll call room, Professor. Whenever you're ready.'

'Yeah, Zito – in a minute, huh?' He took off after Gina. She almost bolted from the coffee machine, then, as though deciding she could not avoid Sonny Crockett

102

forever, pretended like a cup of the squad room's recycled brown turpentine interested her more than anything in the universe.

Not knowing how to start, Crockett opted for breeziness. 'Got everything straightened out on Tubbs, Gina. A little bit of garbage-in, garbage-out with the computer listings.' Then he moved in close enough for her smell to threaten his control. 'You sure made tracks fast this morning – I wasn't even conscious. Woke up with Elvis in my arms.'

She shot out a breath, put down the coffee cup, her lips pressed together whitely. 'I've got nothing to say to you.' Then she stalked off down the corridor. Trudy and some of the others witnessed it. Crockett shrugged for the benefit of his nosy audience, then gave chase.

'Gina – ?' Something had skewed their lovely night together, and he hadn't the dimmest notion what. She increased her walking pace and he doubletimed. 'Gina?' He ducked around her and tried to meet her eyes while back-peddalling down the corridor ahead of her. 'What's wrong – what're you so *mad* about?'

Incredulous, she said, 'Think about it. I'll get back to you.' Then she hung a sudden left into the ladies' room to evade him.

Now the hallway traffic was staring at Crockett. He set his jaw and marched in after her.

'Get outta here,' she said to his image in the mirror. 'You're not supposed to be in here!' Her voice quavered; her composure was thinning fast.

'Gina, look –' he implored, his hands making contact with her forearms, then jerking away as though shocked. 'Look, I didn't *plan* for that to happen last night . . . still, all in all, I think it's pretty terrific that it did . . .' He tried a smile.

'Just sensational, Crockett,' she spat, tears in her

eyes, her vintage Italian temper flaring up. 'Full moon, a boat rocking in the marina, a few drinks too many, soft music . . . a little sudden onboard romance . . .'

'What's so bad about that? It's not a combat campaign or a bust, Gina, I didn't *programme* everything that happened.' The restroom door opened and another female Vice worker took two steps in before Crockett wheeled from the sink and barked '*Do you mind –* ?' sending her recoiling out the door in fright.

Gina ignored it. 'The funny thing is, I almost believed everything you said. Until this morning.' When she saw the confused look on his face she decided to spell it out for him. Men were so dense sometimes. 'Nothing like having a guy roll over at the crack of dawn and murmur his ex-wife's name in your ear to boost your self-image.'

Sonny paled, then blushed hard. 'Oh my God . . .'

'You *are* still in love with Caroline! You *lied* to me!'

'Oh, come on, Gina, I'm sorr – '

'And if you're still in love with her, what the hell was last night all about, anyway?'

'Last night was about you and me.'

'Get a trowel, Crockett – you can spread it even thicker. If you can't make your marriage work –'

He cut her off. It was one thing he *was* good at. 'That marriage *isn't* in the cards, Gina. I thought it might be for us.'

'This is the last situation I wanted to find myself in, Crockett. The "other woman". I don't need it – understand?' Then she shoved past him and banged the door on the way out.

Before he could do anything, she stormed back in for an encore. 'You know – you know what upset me the most? I *let* it happen. Because I *wanted* it to happen. I wanted it in a bad way, Sonny . . . and look what

104

happened.'

*Bang*! She was gone again. Crockett stared at his reflection in the mirror, feeling like a cad. Somewhere in the distance he heard the keening whoop-whoop of a police siren.

Elvis was in the midst of his mid-day sunbath when Tubbs emerged from the galley with an iced tea. He kept an eye on Tubbs in the midst of his reptilian hallucinations; he felt Tubbs had come specifically to steal his blanket.

'My man Elvis,' Tubbs said doubtfully. Then, breaking into a wholly inadequate Presley drawl, he sang, '*You ain't nothin' but an alligator, ah-just ah-cryin' alla time* – you ain't never caught a rabbit and you ain't no friend 'o mine!'

Elvis was not impressed.

Tubbs plunked down, shirtless, near the stern of the *St Vitus Dance* and had himself a good laugh on behalf of Crockett's cassette collection. Rummaging, he counted off the artists: 'Waylon Jennings ... George Jones ... Jimmy Buffet ... Dicky *Betts*? Waylon Jennings ...' He shook his head ruefully. 'Say, Elvis, where's Crockett get his tunes, anyway, the K-Mart forty-nine cent sale? Heh?'

Loyally, Elvis cut loose a bull roar that curdled the urbane smirk on Tubbs' face.

'Ah-hum, yeah, well, you stay cool, Elvis. Have a perch or a pike or whatever the hell it is you eat. You only like white meat, am I right?'

Elvis grumbled. He sounded like Lurch on the old *Addams Family* show.

The phone rang and Tubbs slapped on his Jamaican lilt. '*St Vitus Dance*, you talkin' to Teddy. Hey, de Soto my mon, w'hop'nin?' Translated, this meant *what's happening*? Trini's news turned Tubbs' expression down into a frown. 'No, no, no change in *plan*, mon!'

'Hey no Teddy, *joo* listen to *me*. We're talking a heavy load here, and when Calderone wants to change, he changes. Are you in or out?' Trini gave a new location for a fast rendezvous, to discuss matters not for the phone lines.

'Forty minutes,' said Tubbs. 'I'll be there.'

'I see joo then, mang. And Teddy – don't worry?' The voice was all sweet venom.

'Yeah, don't worry . . .' Tubbs muttered after hanging up. He had brought the rented white Z28 to the marina and figured he could negotiate towards Trini's meeting place in the allotted time. When he ducked downstairs to grab his shirt and check the time, he noticed Crockett's digital clock was gone. Pieces of it were distributed on the bed. The rest had been gobbled up by the only other tenant.

'Elvis, you got no respect for the conventions of time.' He punched in the number of the precinct squad room and waited for his call to be directed. 'Sonny Crockett, please.'

Crockett was in a briefing, and could not be interrupted. Would he care to leave a message?

Pointer in hand, Crockett played schoolmarm to a room-full of the raunchiest-looking characters this side of Miami Detox. They were sprawled around the roll call room in a grungy assortment of T-shirts, beards, sneakers and ball-caps. Zito had the PCP sniffles; Switek slurped on an abused cherry popsicle, and Rodriguez, near the rear of the room, champed on an unlit Dutch Masters cheroot. He looked like a low-rent lawyer covering a bail hearing for a bunch of Modesto Hell's Angels.

Crockett stabbed at key points of the detail map depicting the Southern Florida coastline. 'Switek, Zito and Augustine in the Cobra out of Key Biscayne.' He spot-checked his note cards. 'Hoban, Dibble and Gorman in the thirty-nine foot Cigarette out of Fisher Island. We're not giving the Metro choppers or the Coast Guard cutter our final coordinates until thirty minutes before blastoff. Any questions?'

'Yeah, I gotta question,' said Switek, sneering. 'You roll some *queer* for that shirt, or what?'

Crockett looked down at his Dacron Aloha print. 'No, as a matter a'fact, Ernie, your old lady gave me this shirt . . . and it *wasn't* my birthday.'

Even Rodriguez cracked up laughing with the group.

'Okay, weapons check and final pep rally back here at eighteen hundred, girls; that's Mickey's big glove on the twelve, little glove on the six. Now get outta here.'

As the group dispersed, Gina and Trudy chose that moment to waltz through the squad room . . . to their regret, as they were greeted by a fanfare of wet wolf whistles and overdone frat-boy moaning.

'Oh, grow up, you ass,' Trudy said weakly.

Gina rolled her eyes, and peaked into her mail slot, expecting nothing. She drew out a spin of tissue inside of which was nestled a single, long-stemmed red rose. Spray droplets clung to the petals. Trudy nodded in approval. George Marino squeezed past them both, in order to convey a manila envelope to Sonny, still in the roll call room. Gina saw him watching for her reaction.

She allowed herself a single whiff of the bloom's fragrance, then tucked it carefully into her shoulder bag.

She'd taken the offering with her, and that was enough for Crockett. He slit open the envelope.

First things out were the photo blow-ups. The mystery woman in the flop-brimmed hat seemed closer to Leon de Santis, by the pay phone, in more shots than any other bystanders. Then a slip of paper, listing Leon's contacts. Crockett scanned the column of names and addresses, then looked up in time to catch Lou Rodriguez crossing the squad room. He signalled him inside.

'Excuse me, Lieutenant,' he said, all business. 'Last night I noticed a weird little tattoo on Calderone's Marielito gofer.' He sketched the tattoo in pencil on the back of the envelope, then indicated the fleshy web between his thumb and forefinger. 'Right there. Mean anything to you?'

Rodriguez massaged his chin for a moment. 'Must've gotten it in one of Castro's prisons. It designates a sex offender – homosexual, transvestite, something like that.'

Crockett nodded coolly, assessing his rumpled superior.

Rodriguez caught the probing expression, then turned back with a sigh. 'Okay, Detective, I'm getting tired of being under the Crockett microscope. I boxed a bunch of numbers – got an inside tip on the long-shot triple out at Hialeah last week.'

The dash of truth hit Crockett. 'I bet I know who from, too. You mean to tell me that eighteen grand came from winning a horse race?'

'My stallion came in,' said Rodriguez around his cigar. 'If you're not convinced. I'll show you the slips. But if my wife hears a peep about this, I'm gonna come looking for you, pal.'

Crockett chuckled, accepting the confidence ... then his eyes locked on the name-and-address list provided by the phone company.

Scotty Wheeler's name was on Leon's contact list. Not at his cover address, but at his home phone number.

George came back. 'Almost forgot, Sonny – somebody named Tubbs called for you.'

Panic rushed through Crockett's system. 'When?'

'About twenty minutes ago. Said he had to dash out for a meet with Trini . . . uh, Soho or Soto. It was hard to get the name, he was on that damned radiophone of yours out at the boat, and you know how –'

'Yeah, okay, thanks, George, I owe you a pie.' He rechecked the slip, which did not lie.

If Scotty Wheeler was the leak, then Trini de Soto had called for a meeting, knowing that Tubbs was a cop.

## 9

The Latina hooker was dolled up in a china-blue silk, patterned Spandex, white spikes and phony pearl strings. Her walk was hippy and saucy, drawing a few lewd, hooted comments from the Cuban street workers grunging around in a manhole in the middle of Calle Ocho in Little Havana. Sidewalk hustlers gave her the eye, and two or three of the bolder black pimps offered her employment opportunities. She shrugged them off with experienced moves, from behind wide designer sunglasses and a broad straw sunhat.

She jiggled on down the sidewalk, then stopped to dig a pink Nat Sherman out of her purse. The slight breeze did nothing to ease the sweltering afternoon heat, but it did hobnob the flame of her lighter. She moved towards the windbreak of the nearest alley to light her cigarette, looked up, puffed, and saw Tubbs loitering inconspicuously next to an overflowing trash dumpster about ten yards in.

Tubbs watched the prostitute fire up her Sherman, hoping she didn't spot him, but knowing that if she did, his upscale clothing would make him look like an odds-on-potential customer, slumming it in the Cuban district. Her unabashed mercantile approach made him smile despite the distraction.

'*Bucando fiesta, papasito?*'

Was he looking for a party, a good time? Her voice

sounded laboured, as though from too much partying. Tubbs mustered up a little grace. '*No grácias, mi amor, estoy esperando a un amigo.*'

She nodded regally, signifying her regret. Some other time, perhaps? Then she walked past him, toward the opposite mouth of the alley.

As Tubbs turned his notice back to Calle Ocho, the hooker slipped a chromed .357 Magnum out of her bag and jacked back the hammer, turning to point it at the back of Tubbs' head.

Tubbs heard de Soto's voice growl, '*J*our waiting's over with, dead man.'

With a shriek of tyres and a rasp of disintegrating fibreglass, Sonny's Corvette hit the hump at the far end of the alley and went airborne. It crunched to earth doing a healthy sixty, and ate up the alley in the time it took de Soto to turn and face him on his high heels.

Without a trace of fear, de Soto began plugging shots into the oncoming Corvette. Sonny's head vanished downwards as the windscreen spiderwebbed into fragments. A long furrow jumped from the hood, then another slug lodged in the radiator with a loud *ptang!* sound. A geyser of steam hurried out. Sonny mashed the brakes and sent the vehicle into a speed slide in the cramped passageway.

Meanwhile, Tubbs sprang to the dumpster for cover and yanked a snub-nosed revolver from its compact ankle-holster. While de Soto was filling the Corvette with lead, Tubbs came back up and emptied the little revolver at the Cuban's silk-covered back.

De Soto stopped two bullets before the Corvette broad-sided him, blowing the starboard front tyre and pitching him into the brick wall with enough force to purée his brains. When what was left of him collapsed onto the pavement, his skirt hitched above his waist and blood darkening the blue silk, he was as dead as anything Tubbs had ever seen.

'Crockett!' Tubbs shouted, legging it for the twisted wreck wedged sideways into the alley.

Sonny had stuffed himself diagonally down beneath the crimped-in dashboard. Broken safety glass littered him like snow, and the punctured radiator hissed wetly as the car's engine hitched and died with a sputter.

'Hi there, Tubbs. How's tricks?'

'Very funny . . . ohhh!' He looked over at de Soto and the blood evacuated his face. 'I – I . . .'

Sonny struggled to sit up, his shoulder tendons complaining. But Tubbs looked like he was in trouble, and he pushed himself out of the wreck. 'Tubbs – you okay? You hit?'

He was staring at the revolver in his hand. 'I just . . . Crockett, I've never actually . . . uh . . .'

Sonny knew the signs too well, and used his hands on Tubbs' shoulders to calm and direct him towards the rear of the Corvette so he could throw up with a bit more dignity.

He blotted the images from his mind by super-imposing another image, remembered from the tourist photos taken at the site of Leon's death. Print dress, flop-brimmed hat, wide, round sunglasses to hide most of the face. Hanging around Dino's Dogs. It had been Trini de Soto. Trini was Calderone's latest hitter. He was probably the C4 plastics expert as well as a transvestite and a benzedrine head and an *I Love Lucy* fan. Quite a dossier. Crockett had no doubt that the slugs ballistics would pry out of the radiator of the scrapheap Corvette would match up with the ones that ventilated Leon. Tubbs coughed to clear his throat, and without watching, Crockett handed over his handkerchief. 'You didn't kill Trini, Tubbs . . . I think I did.'

It really didn't matter. Trini was starting to draw flies from the dumpster. He was also drawing gawkers and pedestrians, who swarmed to clog up both mouths of the alleyway.

'Black-and-whites'll be down any second,' said Crockett. Tubbs stared at Trini's limp corpse. His shots had been well-placed. 'That how you planned to do away with Calderone, Tubbs?'

Tubbs didn't take it as an insult. 'I don't know anymore, Sonny. I really don't.'

Crockett's growing rage had nothing to do with Tubbs. They had both become victims. Calderone was running up one mother of a tab to pay. 'Yeah, well, our little interdepartmental leak nearly put you where Trini is now. Personally, I'm glad it's him and not you, *amigo*.'

Less wan, Tubbs said, 'Yeah. Me too.'

Crockett needed half an hour to do something he really hated, and he engineered getting that time mercilessly.

He and Tubbs returned to the Metro station in the Z28. Tubbs drove, indicating his regained calm.

By then, Rodriguez had heard the flood of radio reports relating to the shooting. Sonny let Tubbs do the talking while he gloomed onto a recently-confiscated, ventilated Porsche and a newly installed police band.

By the time Rodriguez got around to asking Tubbs how Trini had been tipped to the fact Tubbs was a cop, Crockett was gone in a squeal of traction radials and a billow of street dust. Tubbs played dumb, buying time for Sonny, who would be coming through on the radio any moment now.

Crockett sat in the parked Porsche. Scotty Wheeler's generous front lawn was littered with children's toys – mostly Karen's, plus whatever was accessible to Bobby Wheeler's motorized wheelchair. When Crockett

113

thought of Bobby's handicap, another piece of the rancid puzzle forming in his brain fell reluctantly in place. Bobby had to be costing Scotty a fortune.

He dragged his Lucky down to the butt and pitched it. Maybe it was a mixup, something to do with Scotty's cover as it related to Leon. Something he hadn't told Rodriguez about. Crockett himself had gone maverick, with no explanation, more times than Rodriguez could count even with his shoes off. The next few minutes would have to be played out with extreme care. Crockett was giving Scotty the benefit of the doubt – perhaps too enthusiastically. He could make no direct accusation. Scotty would have to incriminate himself if he was guilty of being an informer for Calderone.

He felt grim and doom-laden as he walked around the toys. He felt like an executioner when he pressed the doorbell button. And when Scotty Wheeler answered the door, he smiled at the sight of the face of his buddy, Sonny Crockett.

'Hey, Sonny, what brings you to this neck o' the woods?' Scotty had a napkin in one hand. 'Come in, come in, we're just sittin' down to dinner.' Crockett held fast at the threshold of Wheeler's modest suburban home. 'Hey, Donna, look what the wind blew onto our porch.'

Donna, Karen and Bobby looked up from the dining room table. 'Uncle Sonny!' Karen chirped. 'Mom's cookin' spaghetti!'

Donna held a huge bowl crooked against one arm. She always had a ready smile for him. 'Hope you brought an appetite, Sonny.'

'You gonna eat?' said Bobby.

'Naw, not this time, gang.' This easy evocation of the bond of friendship they all shared was crushing Sonny's heart.

'You're gonna be sorry,' Donna said as the kids overdid it, groaning.

'I know,' he said.

Scotty held his hands out. 'What is it, Sonny? What's up?'

Sonny handed over the address book, thumbed open to the page with the numbers. Wheeler's was circled. Scotty did not say anything. When his eyes fell on his own phone number, the guilt was written all over his expression.

Sonny made his gambit. 'If that's not enough, there was a list of payoffs from Trini's pad, too.' He was lying his butt off. 'I think we'd better handle this out in the car. Don't you?'

His voice laden with barely controlled defeat, Scotty played it straight. 'Uh – honey, we've got business. I'll be right back, okay?'

'Don't be long, hon.'

'I won't.'

Sonny said nothing. They sat in the Porsche, watching middle American suburban life go on around them.

Hands on his knees. Scotty stared out the front window. 'Three months behind the mortgage,' he said expressionlessly. 'Damned house, you know? Thirty-six grand for Bobby's medical expenses in '83 alone . . . and me, barely raking in thirty. A crummy thirty thousand a year, for getting shot at by guys who blow that much in restaurants in a month . . .' Scotty's own rage was percolating to the surface. All the compromises he'd made in his life were bubbling blackly up.

Disappointment swelled in Crockett. People didn't realize what kind of coin such compromises ultimately cost them, he thought. And here was Scotty, trying to justify what he'd done. He kept both hands on the wheel, breathing evenly, listening, while his good buddy Scotty dug his own grave with his tongue.

'Six months ago, this guy comes up to me outside of The Gallows Pole, in Little Havana. He hands me a briefcase and says, 'compliments of Mr Calderone'. Nothing else, just... "compliments". I didn't even open the damned thing for over two weeks. It sat there like a ticking bomb. I can't tell you how hard it was, Sonny, you have no way of knowing –'

While Scotty babbled, Crockett calmly picked up the radio mike and keyed it. When he got a clear for transmission, he spoke as though Scotty was still in the house. 'Tell Rodriguez to send backups down to 550 Belinda Street. Tell him I've found the leak.' He replaced the mike. 'How much?' he said, biting the words off in a savage whisper. 'How much to *buy* you, Scotty?'

Scotty considered his newly lost friend, and decided against the easy lie. 'Seventy K American, with a stipend of thirty. The calls from Trini de Soto started about a month later. All they wanted was information... yes or no answers...'

'Information,' said Crockett, his voice dying. Switek and Zito charging in early for the dockside bust had been courtesy of Scotty's information service. All the times that Calderone had slithered through Sonny's fingers like spilled wine – Scotty's fault. Scotty, who played backup on some of the stings that failed. Tubbs had nearly gotten erased an hour earlier, thanks to Crockett's swell buddy Scotty, who hadn't done anything wrong except to pass on a little *information*...

'I... I tried to pull out. At least a dozen times. But it was too late, you know? I never expected anybody to get killed – !'

Now he was grabbling at straws to save his hide, and

116

the sight sickened Sonny – it was the sort of thing he had hoped never to witness. It sliced into his gut like a silver razor. Yesterday he'd been defending Wheeler to Tubbs, while Wheeler was busy selling them both out. 'They changed the game plan on us, Scott. I need to know if the deal's still going down tonight as planned. Where?'

Scotty was sweating, losing it, coming unglued. 'You gotta help me out of this, Sonny. I swear this is the only time! I got a family in there, man, they –'

'Where, Scott?'

'I got fifteen *years* as a stand-up cop! I got two medals of valour!'

'*Where*?'

'*I took a bullet for you once, for God's sake!*'

Wheeler's eyes followed the black-and-white police cruiser as it prowled slowly down Belinda Street, followed by another unit. The lead car pulled up alongside the Porsche. Tubbs was in the passenger seat. Neighbours started peeking out their windows, attracted by the police cars.

'Calderone's running a sports fishing boat out of Keys Marina. The drop-off's upriver.'

Crockett nodded. He'd gotten what he wanted. And it tasted like death and ashes. 'Am I missing something here or what, Scott? I mean, I don't understand this. You were my partner. Caroline and I had you and Donna over to the house for dinner, what, twenty, thirty times each way? Our kids played together. Thanksgivings. Dumb Christmas presents. Birthday parties . . .'

Tubbs had just gotten out of the squad car when he saw Sonny totaly lose it, blowing up in crimsoned-face hate. He grabbed Scotty Wheeler by the throat and began smashing his head against the passenger window, amuck, out of control.

'I trusted you, you bastard, *I trusted you*!' Sonny shrieked, pummelling Wheeler, whom Tubbs saw to be weeping, putting up no resistance.

Tubbs jumped then, knocking back the pilot door and grabbing Crockett by the shoulders, hauling him bodily out of the Porsche. Crockett kicked and flailed and fought to get another shot in at Wheeler. 'Crockett!' Tubbs yelled. '*Crockett*!'

Sonny looked up, tears on his own face, and saw Rodriguez staring at him with an expression of horror.

Tubbs knew better than to ask. All he could do for now was ride along with Sonny, killing the time till the deal went down, providing another human presence to keep Sonny from flying off the handle and maybe, just maybe, soaring the Porsche off a bridge at ninety per. He seemed drained, his last few notches of twine spent. He looped around the other cars northbound on 95 as though they were parked, uncaring, his eyes set in infinity focus, zenning out on the white line.

He occupied himself by taking inventory of the canvas bag stashed in the car, checking out the walkie-talkie set, the flares, the high intensity flashlights. His own sawed-off shotgun was in there, and he took a moment to slot in two deadly cartridges of high-velocity, maximum spread-pattern steel shot, riot charges that would blow the head off an elephant. Sonny was wearing his .45, fully-clipped, with the hammer down on a ninth slug. He had an Ingram Model 10 in the bag with nine full clips, and a long-barrelled .38. Tubbs had added his own artillery to their arsenal.

Crockett's lips worked the whole time, but no words came forth and crystallized. They roared past several police cars but no one offered a chase – that would be Rodriguez on the radio, recommending nobody mess

118

with the Porsche.

Unexpectedly, he said, 'How much time have we got?'

Tubbs checked his watch. 'Twenty-five minutes.'

That decided something in him. He cranked the wheel hard left, ramming across three lanes of traffic and braking in a wheel-locking screech that wasted the tyres and brought the front bumper to a halt four inches in front of an Exxon station phone booth. He jumped out, digging for change.

Feeding Sonny's boy Billy was occasionally a real adventure for Caroline. At six, anything *gooshy* or *squirmy* tickled the devil out of Billy, and though he'd long passed the stage where he had to be fed (and those attendant cleanups were unlovely, she remembered), he was just reaching the juncture where he could truly appreciate a primo gross-out.

*Boom*! Red jello scattered all over the tabletop and quivered like a spreading plague.

'Honey, use the spoon – you know better than that.' At times Billy's table manners were no better than Sonny's. 'I'm gonna have to buy you a feed bag, William Crockett.'

'Oops, not Billy . . . that means I might get it, right?'

She smiled. 'You got it, son.'

He grinned back, glops of jello decorating his teeth. When the phone started ringing, Caroline playfully tossed her napkin at him rather than help him finish the spectacle he had begun.

'Hello?'

'Caroline?'

'Sonny . . .' Odd, him calling just when he was on her mind. She chastized herself by qualifying the thought – *since when is he not on your mind*? – but her concern was

119

instantly roused. His voice was low, almost unnaturally controlled, as though he was stunned. Had he been on another of his disastrous benders? Had there been an accident? The flood of thoughts Caroline experienced illustrated in the harshest way possible the differences that had pried her and Sonny apart.

'I need to know something, Caroline.' He seemed to grope for the right words. Sonny usually just blurted out what was on his mind. 'How . . . the way we used to be together, Caroline . . . I don't mean, uh, lately. But before.' There was another awkward silence. 'It *was* real . . . wasn't it?'

She was whacked, taken aback by the strange question. She took a moment to think of the answer he was seeking, knowing it would not suffice for *both* of them to sound uncertain. 'Yes, Sonny, it was.' It was just like reassuring Billy, when he jolted awake from a nightmare. 'You *bet* it was,' she emphasized with a small smile. 'Sonny – come on, what's wrong.'

'Nothing, Caroline . . .'

She felt a gnawing urge to ask more, to involve herself in whatever his problem was, but she never got the opportunity. When she next spoke she was addressing a dead line.


Sonny hung up the phone.

He supposed he had done the most natural thing. Having just had a deep, longstanding trust betrayed and turned to crap before his very eyes, he had run off, seeking reaffirmation of trust elsewhere. Calling Caroline and dumping it on her had been a cowardly thing to do, he realized now – he had forced her into the position of feeding him straight lines, and that was not what he'd wanted.

She couldn't even hold him now, just hold him.

120

He was absurd, a clown, to think he could ever be in love like a normal person. Even Gina had seen it.

Tubbs assessed him from the car. As Crockett had guided him through his crisis back in Little Havana, so now did Tubbs recognize the danger signals flashing red just beneath Sonny's surface. Sonny had been cheated and smacked hard in the face with the reality of betrayal and human weakness. Disappointed again in the people around him, forced into the corner where he could ultimately trust only himself. That sort of state of mind easily flopped over into suicidal depression, which translated, in a personality like Sonny's, into a suicidal indifference to personal risk. If he tipped over, he'd go after Calderone with guns blazing and everyone would get filled with bullet holes.

He determined that he wouldn't let Sonny down tonight, not after the oddball alliance they'd formed.

He stood up in the seat, poking his head over the windshield. 'C'mon, Sonny, let's wrap Calderone up on schedule. Otherwise Elvis is gonna miss his midnight snacktime, you dig?'

'Right,' he nodded from the booth.

'You sure you're up to this?' Tubbs said, trying to leave nothing out, to be sure of his footing. 'You look a little glazed, and I don't want to go onstage alone tonight.'

'I'm perfect,' he said, his tone less zombiatic now.

'Then let's change for our parts,' Tubbs said, digging out the duffel bag.

'Captain' Max Hart waddled around the deck of the *Smoky Joe*, preparing to cast off on schedule.

The lightweight dope trade in which Hart involved himself had allowed him to refurbish and refit the *Smoky Joe*, his father's motor yacht, for tourist fishing.

With Calderone's help, he scraped by year-to-year, which meant he never had to wear a knit tie again in his life; never had to peddle insurance again. He could live out his seafaring fantasy life in relative peace.

The luminous dial of his diver's watch told him it was showtime. He stumped around to the larboard quarter and saw two dock workers hanging around dockside.

'Hey fellas,' he called down. 'Mind castin' off that line for me?'

Both men wore coveralls. One had a canvas duffel bag. A chocolate and vanilla pair, Hart saw. 'Lucky we caught you in time,' said the white guy with a grin.

Hart's throat tightened. Could be hijackers; it had happened before. Piracy was alive and well, particularly in the narcotics business. 'Oh?' he said, edging sidewise so he could get to the pump shotgun cradled across the wooden arms of a nearby deck chair. 'Why? I forget something?'

'Yeah,' said Tubbs. 'Us.' He levelled the sawed-off shotgun at Hart's head. 'If you're thinkin' of grabbing for that scattergun, my friend, you're gonna wake up staring at the ceiling of the emergency ward.'

Hart got the message loud and clear.

Crockett grinned cruelly. 'Permission to come aboard, sir?'

'Er – you fellas aren't pirates, are ya?' said Hart after a few nautical miles of silence.

'Yeah,' said Tubbs. 'I'm Blackbeard. And this here's Long John Silver.'

'Heaven loves a wise guy,' cracked Crockett.

## 10

The sea was calm, its surface oily-smooth, like slick black glass, glossy and dark and impenetrable. Calderone's eyes frequently held such inscrutable darkness. His eyes told those with whom he dealt very little, offered no clues. He liked it that way. The only person who knew Francisco Calderone at all was Francisco Calderone

His corporate holdings were so enormous that he might have profitably retired from the drug trade years ago, but like Sonny Crockett, Calderone got high on the action – the sheer numbers. The Columbian street urchin in him could not resist flouting the paper authority of the Federales, or spitting in the faces of the Yankee police. The capitalist in him found no action faster than the megabuck sums tossed around for dope shipments. The twenty million dollar deals over which Leon de Santis had waxed orgasmic were not isolated incidents. Nowhere, not even on the no-limit tables at Monaco, was the action faster. There was no risk in pushing chips across baize, and the savvy Columbian street kids rebelled against the notion of something for nothing.

Calderone was much more psychologically complex than the average cliché of the dumb Hispanic elevated beyond his intellect by the power of drug money. Calderone had observed with care, and learned from the example of the recently deposed cocaine king Tony Montana. This caused the formation of an operating credo that by its very extreme nature could not be shared out, even with Calderone's closest confederates – and it also explained why Calderone was standing on a Miami River dock this evening, waiting for Max Hart to show up with his fishing boat, rather than lounging around on his own yacht, getting fat on shrimp canapés while his underlings handled the white stuff . . . and the green stuff.

He sucked on a Turkish-blend cigarette, its smoke sharply contrasting the salt tang of the air on the industrial waterway. On either side of him were waiting a pair of his best shooters – Hector Ruiz, Julio Izquapa, both Brazilians with no sense of humour when it came to guns; Tobe Monteleone, a black muscleman Calderone had brought down with him from New York, and Ray Harris, a rock-jawed ex-FBI man who had been on Calderone's payroll for four years now. Calderone held no racial prejudices, and considered himself an equal opportunity employer. He had, in his nearly fifty years of life, encountered geniuses and idiots of every colour, every creed. He took his talent where he could find it.

Harris was a perfect example of why the efforts of law enforcement agencies to trap Calderone were futile at best and laughable at worst. Calderone bought and sold such men out of petty cash, knowing the rule that governments never adequately compensate those men who make up the enforcement arm of the ruling class. He believed the adage that an honest cop is simply one who hasn't been made a good enough offer. Calderone had watched Harris blow away FBI investigators without a twtich.

You could buy loyalty, but with that purchase came limits, a sort of 'warranty period'. Since Calderone understood this, it was one reason he was still in business and Tony Montana was not. Any man whose head could be turned by proper compensation could also have his head turned again someday . . . no matter how good the pay was. Well-paid men tend to seek other values after a while in the silk. Calderone 'rotated' his staff personally, usually leaving the bodies deep in the Atlantic Ocean. Killing upwards of fifty men had, he thought, made him an excellent judge of human character.

Men were never so eager to please, and never so quick on their feet, as when you first recruited them.

The fact that all of his men were disposable gave Calderone another crucial edge over those who would apprehend him, who believed their job was to spare lives. If it cost Calderone a few warm bodies to escape capture himself, so be it. It was better – and cheaper – than losing cash. His aloof attitude towards life made him appear brutally pragmatic, coldly logical, which in turn inspired awe in those to whom he gave orders. No one who worked for him was close to him, but all respected him . . . even if, for some, it was the respect of the Christian for the lion about to make dinner of him. Corky Fowler, Leon de Santis, Trini de Soto . . . they had all had the peculiar personality warps that made them useful as drug pawns, but all had the drawbacks connected to those personalities that limited their usefulness to boundaries only Calderone could perceive. Thus, losing them was inevitable. Knowing he would lose them in advance allowed Calderone to parlay their loss into gains, mostly of information, or the chess advantages so vital to his survival.

Leon de Santis had arranged for Corky to be blown up. When Corky went to meet his maker, he took some numbskull vice cop with him. When Leon rolled over on Trini and their vice squad informant, Wheeler, Calderone sent Trini to execute Leon on a crowded beach in broad daylight. Both efforts served to strike fear into the hearts of the remaining cops on the squad. They saw that Calderone's justice was thorough and final. Then Trini had been slaughtered... but not before Calderone had discovered just how the cards lay with his supposed buyers tonight. Wheeler had been useful. Now, having outlived his usefulness, he had been discarded. Far better to let his own agency mete out justice to him than to waste time killing him. He would also stand as a demoralizing example to the remaining vice officers.

It was this kind of planning that insured that Calderone, who had never taken a bust, never would.

And after this night, he thought, Miami Vice would be down for the count. He could escalate his operation on the southern coastline as never before. Once they had seen that Calderone could not be beaten, Florida would be wide open. He could commence wiping out the minor-league opposition, expanding his own network, and getting a better grip on the floundering drug-connected Miami corporate system all at once.

He had tried to let the adventurer stuff go, but could not. The street kid in him had compelled him to be in attendance tonight as much as anything. The little Columbian who had never made it past a fourth-grade education would once again kick the butts of underpaid cops with useless college degrees. The corporate magnate would expand his empire, the drug dealer would blot out a few minor irritants, the street kid would get his kicks.

His operatives did not smoke. They wore night-fighting suits and their weapons were flat-blacked so as not to throw glints of reflection that would betray their

126

location. His men were virtually invisible. Their hardware included Ingrams with eighteen-inch glass-pack silencers and pancaking .22 calibre ammo. In a fast *brrriip* of fire they could deliver nearly thirty-five slugs a second from a stretch clip of 177 rounds. Harris was packing his favourite revolver, a .44 Magnum he had nicknamed Stiff Maxie. One slug could blow apart a charging gorilla at forty paces; two shots would sink poor Hart's fishing boat.

Julio, into overkill as usual, wore a bandolero of clips for his own Uzi submachine gun, also combat-silenced, with a bell-shaped flash suppressor making the gun look like a prop from a space war movie. The others also packed their favourite blades and handguns. The four men carried enough assault weight to despose a Nicaraguan dictatorship.

Calderone's own waist holster warmed a Smith and Wesson .38 plated with real Mexican silver. He'd never had to use it against the cops, and he was confident he wouldn't have to pull it out tonight.

He peeled back the cuff of his hand-tailored $150 shirt to expose a $25,000 watch. Where the hell was Hart?

'Hey, Captain Bligh,' Crockett said, getting Hart's attention by tapping his .45 against his shoulder. 'You wouldn't be trying to jerk my partner and I around, now wouldja, by maybe screwing around and wasting enough time to tip off Calderone?'

'Calderone who?' said Hart. 'I don't know anybody named Calderone. I'm willing to take you guys wherever you want to go. You got the guns.'

Crockett was in no mood for this. He pointed the automatic at Hart's head. Tubbs' mouth dropped in surprise. 'Crockett, no!'

127

Crockett pulled the trigger and the blast shook the boat. Hart fell to one knee, clutching at his head.

Tubbs halted. If Sonny had shot the man point blank in the head, that head would be overboard by now.

Sonny knelt with a skewed smile, and shoved the bore of the gun into Hart's ear before cocking the hammer. 'Now,' he said calmly. 'You ready to lose the other eardrum, or do we play ball? And don't ask me to repeat myself, scuzzwad.'

Hart, who had felt the bullet whizz right past the bridge of his nose as his left eardrum exploded, decided that playing ball was an excellent option. His head was ringing like a Chinese brass gong. The sticky track of blood dribbling from his ear felt cool in the night air.

'Jesus, Sonny...' Tubbs said, aghast.

'I thought you said you were up to this, New York,' Sonny growled. 'Do I have to handle everything by myself? Are you gonna fall apart on me, too?'

Tubbs put his gun away. 'I'm cool. But are you straight?'

'Who cares,' Sonny said. He yanked Hart around by the arm that the man used to clutch his ear. 'Where's the rendezvous, wise guy? I'll drive.'

'The old Tokay pier,' mumbled Hart, his vision blurred by the pain in his ear. 'Off the industrial waterway, near what used to be the maintenance area for the shipyard.'

Sonny showed Hart towards the rear of the yacht. 'Don't look so disapproving, Tubbs. He's not permanently damaged. You keep an eye on him. We're gonna be late.'

'You know where we are?'

'Roughly. Okay, Captain – you got a speed contingency on this tub in case of pursuit?'

'Yeah. Starter button's the blue one right in front of

128

you. Kicks in an auxiliary engine for an extra five hundred horsepower or so.' Hart sat there, deflated, like a schoolkid caught misbehaving.

Crockett thumbed the button and they all felt the extra engine grumble to life within the bowels of the yacht. 'It's an edge,' Crockett conceded. 'We've gotta get there first, or else Rodriguez and the backups and the Coast Guard and everybody else is gonna drop out of the sky and wind us up with two fistfuls of nothing."

Realization dawned in Hart. 'Geez – you guys are *cops*!'

'You sound relieved,' said Tubbs.

'You bet your butt, young man. I thought you were dope hijackers. I was looking forward to a nap at the bottom of the bay, y'know?'

Air whistled out between Tubbs' teeth. This squirmy little squid had realized he wasn't going to die, and knew that Calderone's lawyers would get him off the smuggling rap without so much as thirty seconds of cell time. If he'd known a moment earlier, he might not have spilled the location of the pier to Sonny, knowing that cops wouldn't shoot him. Now Tubbs felt like blasting Hart himself.

'What's Calderone got waiting for us?' he said.

Hart played both sides, figuring to ease his burden of guilt. 'He's got four boys with him. That's all I know.'

'Awful lot of guys to carry one suitcase full of money,' Sonny observerved.

'But just enough guys to cart away two dead detectives,' said Tubbs, 'and dump 'em in the drink wearing concrete boogie shoes.'

'Make sure our hardware is ready to roll,' said Sonny. 'Now I'm scared that we didn't bring enough ammo.'

'I'm a good shot,' said Tubbs. 'My momma taught me never to waste bullets.'

'I noticed,' Sonny grinned, referring to Tubb's well-placed shots during the debacle with Trini de Soto.

'Calderone knows who we are,' Tubbs had to assume. 'We don't know how much Wheeler spilled.'

'Have to figure he knows everything. But he'll play the fake long enough to make sure we're in his sights.'

'Wonderful. That gives us maybe five seconds to get a fix on the shooters.'

'Hey, New York – you want a cushy assignment, go back to Armed Robbery.'

'You're a million laughs, Crockett.'

'And you, Captain.' Crockett added for Harts benefit, 'You bring us in as though we're perfectly kosher. Nothing beyond SOP. And stay on the boat unless you want to get something shot off.'

'Aye aye, sir,' Hart saluted grimly, his head still reverberating.

'I don't know,' muttered Crockett. 'Looks like we don't stand a chance either way. What's to stop Calderone from potshotting us as soon as we grin for him? It's not gonna *work* if he knows we're the heat, Tubbs!'

'It'll work,' Tubbs returned with flat sureness. 'Two reasons – first of all, as far as he knows, the setup bread is the real McCoy. He stands to make ten million bucks just for spending a quiet evening scratching two cops . . . that's a pretty piece o'change, and he's not averse to bumping people off for less.'

'The Columbian had a hefty hit list just in Florida,' nodded Sonny. 'Nationwide he's probably killed off a lot more for a lot less.'

'And he's not going to give the word until we hand the cash over . . . stop me if I err.'

'What's the second reason?'

'Raphael,' said Tubbs. 'He knew Rapheal and Jake

Bartamas were cops. He went through with the deal, all the motions... then at the last minute he offed everybody.' Tubbs recalled the look of surprise on his brother's face, the suddenness with which things happened once the deal had been 'concluded'. Calderone's ego made him elongate the delicious charade as far as he could.

'Comin' up on Tokay pier. What now?'

'Drop speed,' said Hart. 'Wait for 'em to signal you with the headlights. Two blinks.'

'Take the helm,' commanded Sonny. 'We locked and loaded, New York?'

Tubbs unnecessarily rechecked the loads in his shotgun, smacked a full clip into the Ingram, and broke open the cylinders of the long-barrelled .38 and his own .357. Tucked into his belt were speed-loaders for the latter pistol, and he had a pocketful of shotgun shells. Sonny drew only one extra clip for the Ingram; two for his .45. He dropped out the unused clip from his pistol and replaced it with a fresh, in order to keep the bonus shot in the chamber, plus eight, replacing the bullet he'd fired past Hart's head.

'Show-time,' he said.

Caldrone had just checked his wristwatch when he became aware of the low grumbling of the *Smoky Joe*'s engines. He and his shooters squinted into the inky darkness. In the distance, a large motor yacht cut engines and drifted, its running lights out.

Calderone snapped his fingers, pointing. It was his standard signal for action. Hector Ruiz trotted over to one of the two Jeep four-wheel-drive vehicles parked to either side of Calderone's funeral-black Mercedes. All three cars were pointed towards the water.

'*Luces, pronto!*'

Hector hit the Jeep lights and the rim of the pier lit up once, twice.

On the *Smoky Joe* Hart turned to Sonny from the helm. 'I have to blink back. It's standard procedure. Otherwise they'd open fire, thinkin' this was a narc boat.'

'Or maybe that's what they'd think if you *did* blink the lights,' hissed Tubbs. 'Sonny – he might be setting us up!'

'One way to find out,' said Crockett. 'Blink back. And remember you'll be the first one out of the boat if I get the faintest whiff of trouble, Cap'n.'

'Yessir,' Hart grovelled doggedly, signalling.

Tubbs saw Crockett's reasoning. If the signal was not required, Calderone and company would most likely pile into their cars and run for it. Sticking around to shoot it out with vice cops who already had the drop on you didn't make sense. If their own cover was blown by the signal, they stood a better chance on the boat.

Nothing provocative happened. Hart was playing it straight; he just wanted to get this night over with.

The *Smoky Joe* manoeuvred in and bumped softly against the dock.

'What now?' said Crockett.

'Signal one blink with your flashlight, then hold up the Haliburton case so they can see it.'

Tubbs worked the flash and lifted the case.

'*Oigan, idiotas,*' Calderone snapped at Hector Ruiz and Tobe Monteleone. '*Muevanse!*'

The two men moved quickly across the darkened pier for the boat. Tubbs could now see the automatic weapons they were toting. 'Ingrams,' he said to Sonny.

'Stay cool. Let 'em board.'

Hector and Tobe were halfway up when they were dragged the rest of the way over by Tubbs and Crocket, hiding just below the rail. Hector dropped his gun and it slid across the deck. A flurry of punching and chopping later, both shooters were more or less groggy and senseless.

'Get your butt belowdecks, Cap'n. And don't come up.'

Gratefully, Hart scuttled through and shut the galley hatch.

'Use that slap-happy dude as a shield, Tubbs,' said Sonny. 'And stand up. Here we go.'

## 11

The instant the men on the pier saw the advance guard set rudely yanked over the side, they snapped alert, their lethal weaponry already cocked and ready to spray death all over the waterfront.

Calderone seemed prepared for this strategic action, almost blasé. '*Mantenete firme,*' he whispered, and his two best men held fast.

'*Alto vatos, es la policia!*' Crockett shouted towards them.

He was going by the book, all right, noted Tubbs. They had to identify themselves if what went down here tonight was to be lawsuit-proof. And Calderone would have a whole stable of lawyers to sniff out any screw up they might make.

It was not in Tubbs' plan, however, for Calderone to survive this evening's fun.

He spotted the shooter on the right trying to take aim, unable to get a clear shot around the body of his stupified comrade. '*Un movimiento y los hago como pasta de frijoles!*' Tubbs yelled, threateningly, he hoped.

'One move and they're *bean* paste?' said Crockett, sidewise, unbelievingly. 'This isn't a *movie*, Tubbs . . .'

'You're right,' he said. ''Cos it looks like the good guys aren't showing up on schedule. Where the hell's Rodriguez?'

'Still on Daylight Savings Time, I guess. We're just

gonna have to stand 'em off.'

'*It's just these two!*' screamed Tobe, before Crockett laid the butt of the .45 into his temple in response. He grunted and sagged.

'Great,' sighed Crockett.

It was a royal Mexican stand-off, tense and time-elongating. The shooters looked downwater to try and see any backup boats, and spotted none.

'*Apartanse, hombres,*' whispered Calderone. '*Julio, a la izquierda. Coje el tipo negro.*' Then he turned to Ray Harris, the rock-jawed ex-FBI man. 'Ray – to the right. At my signal shoot the white one – through Tobe.'

Harris nodded. He and Izquapa waited for the signal to blast the vice cops away by shotting through their partners – their *former* partners.

Another fifteen seconds ticked agonizingly off. 'Looks like we're up that world-famous creek,' said Crockett. 'No oars.'

Tubbs had his shotgun trained in Calderone's direction, trying to support the semi-conscious Hector and point his weapon at the same time. Hector's Ingram gun lay on the deck, out of reach.

Crockett held Tobe in a half-nelson, doing the same, his own Ingram targeted on a right-to-left track that would kill Harris first, then Calderone, in a sweeping motion, in case he himself got hit in the first split seconds of automatic weapons fire.

Calderone seemed unruffled. He was the only one not sweating.

Harris lowered his Ingram and pulled Stiff Maxie from his shoulder holster. The high-velocity .44 Magnum slugs would plough through Tobe's body like pound cake, assuring him of a strike on the cop behind Tobe. But accuracy was reduced at this range. He weighed variables and chose the monster pistol anyway.

135

Julio Izquapa held his muffled Uzi steady. There was only half a torso for him to aim at, and he had to account for distance and the rocking motion of the yacht. In his mind, Hector, his fellow Brazilian, was already dogfood.

All eight men – Captain Hart included – heard the chuddering noise of the incoming police chopper. Calderone's men glanced up and saw a brief flash of bobbing sky search-light.

That was it. Crockett shoved Tobe violently forward and brought up the Ingram in a single fast motion. Tubbs, at the same instant, did likewise, hauling up his shotgun. Hector and Tobe went over the side face-first and weaponless.

Ray Harris unleashed the first slug, and if Crockett hadn't half-stepped to point the Ingram at him, his head might've been torn off. Instead the slug bit a pound-and-a-half chunk out of the main mast next to Crockett's face, causing him to hit the deck. His first squeeze-off flew into the sky.

Tubbs triggered both barrels dead ahead, but by then their adversaries were scattering for the cars. Already, he could no longer see Calderone. A roar, a flash, and grey smoke. He heard the pellets patter into the Mercedes and Jeeps. Then, as Julio opened up on them with the Uzi, he ducked below the side to reload the shotgun.

The .44 bellowed again, and a hunk of *Smoky Joe*'s side as big as a serving platter was punched out above Sonny's lowered head. '*Damn*!' he winced.

Quickly, he crabwalked several feet towards the bow, then popped up like a shooting gallery target and blew about a hundred slugs towards Harris. The front of the Jeep on the far right disintegrated behind the hail of bullets. Chrome moulding leapt into the air, twinkling. The headlights burst, scattering pebbled safety glass.

136

The metal pinged as the bullets left dozens of hammer-dents in the vehicle's hide. The sheer chaos of the salvo kept Harris' head down while Sonny moved. Then the Ingram clip hollowed and ran dry.

Harris scrambled for better cover, firing three more shots. They went wild.

The Metro chopper swung into view above, hanging in the air and putting the spotlight on the trio of parked cars. Crouched behind one of the Jeeps, Julio grimaced into the severe glare and gave the helicopter half a clip from the Uzi. Sonny heard the carbon-arc light explode, its last beams whipping hard right as the chopper wheeled away and retreated.

Julio clamped his eyes shut against the blazing after-images in his inner eyelids. Effectively blinded for a few seconds, he spent the rest of his clip in the direction of the boat.

Thirty new holes appeared in *Smoky Joe*'s port side as the heavier-calibre slugs ripped through.

Ray Harris laid down cover fire with his Ingram while Julio reloaded.

'Sonny!' shouted Tubbs. 'Look out, man!'

Sonny spun in time to see Tobe clambering over the starboard rail, grabbing for one of the fallen machine guns. He drew the .45 automatic left handed and plugged two slugs into the black man's chest, then kicked him in the face. His arms swanned back as he fell and hit the surface of the water in a clumsy splash. He gargled seawater and this time he sank and stayed down.

Tubbs turned his attention back to Julio as Harris reloaded his Ingram. Then a dripping hand clamped around his mouth and twisted his head wrenchingly to the left. He fell on his back and before he could sort things out, Hector was pinning him down and strangling him.

'Tubbs! Get outta the way!' Crockett tried to draw a bead on Hector's back, then had his hands full dodging fire from Julio.

They couldn't stand off all night. Rodriguez would show up – by dawn, maybe – or the shooters would run out of ammo. Maybe thirty seconds had passed since the first shot had been fired. The entire gunfight at the infamous OK Corral, Crockett knew, had taken a grand total of forty-five seconds.

Tubbs swung the shotgun and missed Hector's skull by a quarter-inch. Hector freed one hand to grab for the gun, and when he did Tubbs jerked the .357 out of his own belt, jammed it into Hector's stomach, and pulled the trigger convulsively until the pistol was empty. Hector fell on his head, flailing, trying to keep his own insides from flying out.

The engine of the Mercedes coughed and caught. The headlights flared on.

'Tubbs! The car!'

Tubbs struggled to his feet, oxygen-starved. He stumbled, woozy from the squashed windpipe, and dropped his shotgun.

Sonny pushed in close to him with the other enemy Ingram and emptied the clip towards Calderone's car. The headlights shattered and the pier went dark again. In the distance, Crockett finally saw the red-white-blue flashings of at least four cars, gumballs and flashbars winking madly, as they piled up the access road, making a beeline for Tokay pier.

Julio and Harris were doing it right, putting out an almost uninterrupted barrage of fire.

The relatively small calibre of the Ingram did little to impede the Mercedes at that range. Tubbs shook off his momentary drunk and discharged both barrels of the shotgun, then pulled his .357 and fired simultaneously with Sonny's .45 calibre shots.

With a lung-deflating *whummp*! the gas tank of the nearest Jeep let go, dealing out burning parts in every direction and knocking Julio on his can, his coat afire. A bright orange mushroom cloud bloomed above the vehicle. Return fire had stopped for the moment.

Sonny kept firing until his second clip was gone. One of the Mercedes' hubcaps jigged madly, a terminal dent in its middle, and it wobbled away from the car like a fractured Frisbee. Tyre and tread came apart in a way that insured Calderone was driving nowhere this evening. The cabin windows were sprinkled with stars of powdered glass. It was possible the cabin itself was armoured – but what would Calderone do now that his wheels had been cut out from beneath him?

'Jump,' said Sonny. 'It's now or never!'

Tubbs realized what he meant, and hurled himself over the side. He had just snapped a fresh ring into his .357 and was digging for two more shotgun shells. He dropped one when his feet hit the pier. It rolled off the edge and into oblivion.

Crockett had burst into a flat-out fullback charge across the open zone of fire, the Ingram in one hand and the .45 in the other. Tubbs saw Harris poke his head up from behind the undamaged Jeep, and fired blindly at him until the .357's hammer snapped on empty brass. His shots were close enough to keep Harris pinned until Sonny could dive for the cover of an industrial crane mount left over from the pier's shipyard service days.

Sonny landed rolling and crashed into the leeward side of the mount. He was surrounded by solid, rusting iron. Immediately he checked back for Tubbs, saw him still standing by *Smoky Joe*, and cocked the Ingram in case Harris decided to play trench soldiers some more and fire on the man out in the open.

The engine on the Mercedes sputtered and conked out.

Sonny gave the other Jeep a short burst, to make Harris hug the ground. Perhaps he was out of ammunition.

Tubbs was kneeling near one of the mooring posts, the only available cover. He had reloaded the shotgun now, and was searching his belt for another load ring for the .357. That was when Sonny turned and saw the treacherous Captain Bligh, aka Max Hart, getting to his feet on the deck of the *Smoky Joe* and aiming a war souvenir Luger at the back of Tubbs' head.

'*Tubbs* – !'

The young black detective didn't bother to look and see what the danger was. He instantly flattened and rolled, causing Hart to tack on him as he moved, winding up on his back, facing the boat, with his shotgun braced against the dock. He snapped both triggers without cocking, and Sonny saw the way Hart flew to pieces, doing an end over and completely off the starboard side of the yacht, as Tubbs' double discharge pitched him into the air. His deck shoes flew off in different directions as he belly-flopped into the drink and went down to meet Neptune.

Then a huge, ugly wad of lead flattened into the steel a foot away from Sonny's shoulder, making a knuckle-sized crater in the metal, and Sonny knew Harris was alive and kicking, trying to eliminate him with his Magnum, Stiff Maxie. Stopping one of those slugs with his body would be like trying to catch a cannon shell in a baseball glove, Sonny knew, and he stuck the Ingram over the lip of thick dockside iron and fired blind.

Tubbs booked for Sonny's position, high-stepping when bullets started chasing his feet, gouging foot-long splinters out of the dock. Calderone had emerged from the Mercedes with another Uzi. He was silhouetted against his car by the flames from the Jeep. Beyond that was a smoking hulk that was once Julio – his fire was out, but his body was not moving.

'Okay, Coach,' Tubbs said as he landed feet-first against the steel, stopping his mad momentum. 'What now?'

'Five down, two to go.'

As Sonny spoke, Harris retreated to the Mercedes, and together he and Calderone backed towards the warehouse behind them.

'The other Jeep must be kaput,' said Sonny. 'Make for it after they've gained a few more yards.'

They kept their heads down and the firing stopped. 'Go!'

They charged together. Calderone and Harris were nowhere to be seen. When they reached the Jeep without incident, Sonny swore again. 'They're holing up inside.'

'There's only two of them,' said Tubbs, eager.

'Try not to be so anxious to get us killed, huh?'

'Standard one-two. Let's go before they have time to plan an ambush.'

'You reloaded, New York?'

'Of course. You?'

Crockett hadn't seen him, but knew he had. He reclipped the pistol and the Ingram, and nodded.

The service door hung a quarter of the way open. It was of corrugated steel, with a wooden beam X through its centre. Inside it was like a huge atrium, open in the middle, but with several floors of catwalks and steel steps circumventing the interior, and all of it congested with junk, old packing material, rotting shipping supplies, rats' nests, barnacle rot and mildewed pilings.

Calderone wouldn't fire on them once they came

through the door, thought Crockett – that would give away their position too quickly. They braced the door on either side. Their eyes met – a near perfect team. At a nod they both knew Tubbs would kick the door, Crockett would duck in and cover the unknown space while Tubbs covered him. And so would begin the peculiar but effective leap-frogging technique used to make slow progress in hostile territory.

Crockett's muscles were like high-tension wires, his nerves like guitar strings. He had opened his mouth to say the word *now* when a volley of fire behind them froze them back to the spot.

They pivoted just in time to see Julio Izquapa fold up, like a snail hit by cold water, as bullets perforated him and forced him to release his hold on the Uzi he had trained on their backs from his prone position behind the smouldering Jeep. The weapon rattled to the ground without going off.

Fifteen yards back stood Lou Rodriguez, his service revolver still wisping blue smoke, a Tac squad member to either side.

Crockett gave Lou a flat-handed signal.

'What's he want, Lieutenant?' asked the jumpsuit-clad SWAT man.

Lou shook his head resignedly. 'He wants us to hold back and cover the outside of the warehouse. Damned hot dog.'

'But we should go in as support –' protested the team leader, a speed-freak Aryan with arctic blue ice-chip eyes. His name was McCullough, like the chainsaw, and Lou could see the frustrated bloodlust in the man's android eyes. McCullough cradled his M-16 lovingly against one forearm. The rest of his men milled around waiting for new orders, disappointed that the dockside firefight was already history before they'd rolled up.

'Hang back,' said Lou. 'It's just one guy; I doubt if he's gonna try to take on all of us. Let Crockett and Tubbs bring him out.' He gnawed on his cigar, and looked at the men around him. 'Anybody around here happen to have a match...?'

## 12

The interior of the airy structure held a bilge odour, and Tubbs' vision swam as he tried to adjust. Crockett stood spread-legged to the left, his Ingram ready to cut apart anything that flinched.

Tubbs had stuffed the .357 back into his waistband and favoured the shotgun. It would be easier to track the flashes of gunfire in this place . . . but the hollow-steel acoustics were a handicap. Gunfire might seem to be coming from everywhere at once.

Crockett whipped the flat of his hand up. Both men stood still as if petrified.

There was a small, dainty noise – *tink, tink, tink*. They both heard it.

Crockett's whisper barely disturbed the air. 'I'll lay odds they're headed for the roof.'

'What for?'

'Calderone could pick us off if he wanted to, anytime. But he wants to buy time. To get to the roof of the warehouse.'

Tubbs shook his head in the negative, almost invisible in the damp blackness. He still didn't get it.

'Why do you think Calderone spent so much time trying to start his Mercedes after I'd blown off the wheel?'

It clicked. 'Reinforcements? Or rescue,' said Tubbs. More troops were unlikely since a whole SWAT squad had just checked in outside. The evening had transcended a mere dope gunfight, bust and shutdown. Now Calderone had to escape.

'We can't wait around for safety's sake,' breathed Crockett. 'By the time we get to the roof, he'll be gone. He probably called for a helicopter on his CB.'

It stood to reason. Calderone had millions in personal wealth. Even in the matter of saving his own hide, he was proceeding in a ruthlessly businesslike fashion. He had not retreated until the odds between his forces and Crockett's had been evened, two for two. He spent his shooters like chessmen, trying to gain an advantage for each one lost – even if that advantage was only an extra second to duck, or a diversion allowing him to flee into a convenient chuckhole. He was oily and experienced. He had never been so much as busted on peripheral charges, but if he had, there would have been a battery of attorneys and a bank-full of currency to free him. The cost of this little inconvenience had not yet matched the potential cost of such a legal machination . . . and so, Calderone was still trying to get away.

'While he beats it for the roof, he's stationed his last shooter between us and him,' finished Crockett. 'Smart. Doesn't leave us a second to inhale.'

'So let's go.'

Crockett huffed out a breath of disbelief. Tubbs sure seemed in a hurry to get shot up. In keen contrast to the episode with Trini de Soto, Tubbs had been the total professional during the waterfront shootout. At least Crockett felt he did not have to fret about his rear end being covered by a greenhorn. Tubbs would come through when the blasting started.

Leap-frogging, guns forward, they made for the ground-floor stairway.

It was disused, of extremely rusty metal. It creaked.

'You sure this thing is, uh ... safe?' said Tubbs.

Crockett took two steps up, feeling the rickety construction swaying gently with his weight. 'Absolutely not,' he said. 'Come on.'

Their shoes crunching rust to maroon powder, they eased up the stairway, feeling like jungle hunters nailed on a rotten rope bridge.

A brilliant white-yellow starburst of light broke out from the second floor level, accompanied by the blatting stutter of Harris' Ingram gun. Slugs peppered the stairs two feet behind Tubbs and Crockett, skimming off the steel, leaving tracer-like, sparking patterns on the still, wet air. One burst, then silence.

Crockett scrambled for the top of the ladder-like stairway. Tubbs flattened, hugging the decayed metal, hoping the railing in front of his face would deflect any errant shells. This was smarter procedure than it appeared. Momentarily blinded by his own fire, the shooter above them would not be able to get a fix on their location until they made another noise. He would also assume both men were together.

Sonny tracked both left and right from the point where he saw the gunfire light up the catwalk, and salted the dark area liberally with bullets from his own Ingram. The warehouse was temporarily drowned in the crazy cartoon sound of the bullets ricocheting everywhere, bouncing and glancing from surface to surface inside the all-metal building.

Harris nailed Sonny's position and fired. As lead pattered all around him, flaring meteorically like thrown, lit matches, he dived headfirst out towards the catwalk. The trick was to fire, then shift position as fast as you fired.

Sonny nearly performed a one-storey swan dive when he overshot the catwalk and was carried under the rail by his own momentum. His foot scraped across the catwalk and he clawed madly with his right arm, latching onto the rusting rail just as gravity started to pull him earthward. He lost his grip on the Ingram and it fell, spinning, like an autumn leaf made out of cast lead, to break apart on the concrete floor twenty-five feet below. An involuntary curse escaped from him when he thought he was going to do the parachute bit.

Harris tacked on him and put a few rounds into the general area, feeling out Crockett's position. For that instant, Crockett was a sitting duck, half-off, half-on the catwalk.

Tubbs gave one barrel of shot to Harris' assumed position. The shotgun kicked against his arm and the roar sounded like a volcano touching off. A lethal cloud of pellets flew off to keep Harris quiet for a few more vital seconds.

Crockett, pawing and groping, found the catwalk and dragged himself up onto it, rolling onto his back and ripping the .45 free of its holster.

When Harris fired another burst at Tubbs, spending his clip, Tubbs let him have it with the second barrel. In the steel and concrete warehouse the reports were truly brain-numbing. While everything settled down, Tubbs ran for the landing.

'Hey man!' he shouted clearly. 'The place is surrounded by cops! Calderone's throwing you to the dogs; he doesn't give a *damn* about you, man, and your ammo can't hold forever!'

Crockett had no idea of what Tubbs was up to, but used his entreaty as cover noise to make his way down the catwalk. Then it occurred to him that Tubbs was bellowing precisely so Crockett could advance – he knew Tubbs didn't care zilch for keeping some Calderone lackey from marrying up with his tombstone.

Tubbs was buying him room to move at the risk of getting shot. Carefully, quickly, Sonny made like a cat, and catwalked.

'I mean, you don't wanna die for *nothing*, now do ya, dude?'

The response that Harris barked towards Tubbs was something that Tubbs defintitely had no desire to repeat to his mother during a Sunday afternoon phone call. He also heard the sound of Harris dropping an empty clip and slapping in a full one – the sort of sound that tells intelligent men that the time for negotiation is past.

Tubbs moved as Harris fired again. His back to an iron girder, the old rivets digging into his spine as he reloaded, plugging his final two shells into the shotgun and drawing his .357.

*BBrrrriip*! Harris fired on Sonny's last known position, not yet realizing that Sonny was standing twenty paces away on the catwalk.

Sonny's lip curled, and he assumed a spread-legged firing stance with the .45. As Harris turned and spotted him, Sonny fired mechanically, efficiently, one-two-three-four.

The first slug dented the Ingram beyond usability and booted it from Harris' grasp. The second caught him high in the right shoulder as he pivoted to pull out Stiff Maxie. His arm caught fire and shorted out with pain, his fingers brushing the butt of his pet Magnum but not retaining enough nerve-sense or coordination to grab it. The ex-FBI man had been knocked backward, but remained, almost impossbily, on his feet after taking the bullet. The third shot took care of that, kicking him backwards as it ploughed through his upper torso, shattering his right collarbone and nearly clipping the top off a lung. It tore away an exit wound as big as a beer bottle bottom, spoiling Harris' night-fighting suit. He fell down and went *boom* on the catwalk, his left hand clutching at the pumping mess the two slugs had made of his upper right side.

The fourth shot careened into the darkness and ricocheted loudly before dying.

'Tubbs!' Sonny shouted as soon as Harris collapsed. 'You okay?'

'Yeah, I think so. No holes in me yet. You get him?'

'Dead bang,' affirmed Sonny. 'Get up here.'

Tubbs clambered down the catwalk as Sonny approached the fallen shooter. What happened next was a flurry of confusing activity not sorted out until much, much later.

At the sound of a doorway on the upper level clanking back, Tubbs shouted, 'Sonny, look out!' and gave Crockett a gung-ho shove that spilled him on top of Harris – and nearly off the edge of the catwalk again – just as Calderone opened fire with his pistol.

The first shot scratched off the rusty railing inches from Tubbs' right hand, and he spun. There was nowhere to duck to, and Calderone's third shot caught him in the middle of his left forearm. His body seized up in broiling pain and he let go of his shotgun, which clattered on the catwalk at his feet.

Three more shots, all blind-fire misses, and the door slammed shut again.

When Sonny tumbled face-to-face with Harris, he found the wounded man doggedly trying to pull his .44, Stiff Maxie, left-handed. There was no time to draw and shoot, but there was time for him to bounce the canon-like barrel off Sonny's forehead as a final, last-gasp gesture of defiance.

Sonny went 'Oww, god!' He lost the lock on his elbows and floundered.

Tubbs had pulled his .357 to return fire at Calderone,

but managed to shift despite the stabbing throb of agony in his recently perforated arm and cocked the gun to blow Harris' head into squash.

Harris, obviously a man on the way out, lifted his head an inch off the grated platform and hissed, 'It ... could be ... *bloody* ... ahh!' Then he passed out and his head struck the metal again with a low bong.

Tubbs dipped, retrieved the shotgun. Sonny was still moving so he seemed okay. He stepped over Sonny and Harris and ran as best he could for the next stairway, which would lead him to the roof door Calderone had fired through.

Six shots. If Calderone was packing no reloads, his wad was shot.

Sonny heard Tubbs take off, but his vision was a black-and-white-TV static blur. Damned shooter had pegged him right on the temple, and had brought blood. Then he had blacked out so Sonny could not have the satisfaction of shooting him with a clear conscience.

He tried to stand, weaved, and crashed into the catwalk railing, coming close to another swan dive into the cement. No way.

'Tubbs!' he shouted, holding his head to keep his brains from leaking out. Assuming, he thought, there were any left. Tubbs had run off to face Calderone, and that meant Sonny was never going to feel the satisfaction of handing Calderone over to the authorities. Not if Tubbs' favourite sawed-off equalizer had anything to say about the whole event.

The catwalk ahead drifted into soft focus. He patted his armpit for the .45, then slowly, laboriously, using both hands to feel his way towards the stairs, he began to step like a blind man towards the roof.

Tubbs heard Sonny shout but ignored it. The yell

meant Sonny was all right – injured perhaps, but not requiring his presence for another try at a brink-of-death statement, as Raphael had tried, and failed.

He kept his pulsating arm stiff and at his side.

His brain was peaking with recall, revving, as his body jumped with adrenalin. He felt Raphael's head go slack in his arms, and felt the dampness of his brother's blood. He imagined Calderone nodding his head, signalling his button men to open fire on the *Smoky Joe* tonight, just as he had given the nod to initiate Raphael's death, like some weird, omnipotent toad king with a Columbian accent and barely five feet of height.

He had murdered Raphael, Corky Fowler, Leon, and Sonny's partner Eddie Rivera. He had destroyed Trini de Soto and Scotty Wheeler. He had fouled the waters of the entire East Coast and made law enforcers up and down the Atlantic seaboard look like children with cap guns and severe learning disabilities. Rodriguez had mentioned at least seven other Calderone murders in Florida alone ... and there were probably at least as many duplicates of Calderone, killing just as many people, becoming millionaires by drugging millions more, and dirtying the whole system by hiding behind lawyers, renting policemen at bargain-basement rates, and buying judges wholesale.

*Nothing personal, Mr Calderone*, Tubbs thought as he kicked the metal door open and levelled the shotgun.

The diminutive drug kingpin was not lying in ambush beyond the door. Carefully, Tubbs stepped out.

The air and the warehouse had begun to vibrate with a subtle humming that resolved into clarity as Tubbs came outside. It was the eggbeating sound of approaching helicopter rotors, either the pickup Sonny had speculated on, or another Metro police chopper.

Tubbs hadn't brought his tourist camera, and so did not wish to wait idly around to find out which answer was the one that would win the prize.

He made out the red and blue running lights hovering in the night sky, growing larger. The whirlybird was coming in straight on course from somewhere out in the bay. He didn't know enough about Dade County's chopper pads to know if a directional fix made any sense.

One, two brief flashes from a hand-held pocket light. Calderone stood on the extreme west end of the roof, signalling the chopper towards him. Rodriguez and his men were on the other side of the building, blissfully unaware of Sonny's conjecture.

Calderone had nowhere to run when Tubbs sped up behind him. He turned and regarded the detective's shotgun with disinterest, then turned back to continue signalling the helicopter.

Teeth meshed in fury, Tubbs rammed Calderone in the back with the chopped-off dual bore of the weapon.

Calderone turned back around. 'What's *your* problem?' he said with utter contempt.

Tubbs swung the barrel, knocking the flashlight from the smaller man's grasp and over the side. Just as the approaching chopper dropped a rope ladder, Tubbs cocked the first barrel and dusted the underside of the helicopter with a roaring blast.

The bird wheeled about in the air and quickly retreated the way it had come. SWAT men, brought by the sound of the discharge, came running around to the west side, four storeys below Tubbs and Calderone.

Calderone had the lip of the roof to his back, and a not-quite-sane Tubbs an inaccessible five feet away. He cracked a lopsided smile, held his empty pistol for Tubbs to see, and dropped it at his feet. He stretched his hands into the classic position. 'Come on, you four-hundred-buck-a-week cop. It's getting late. You can arrest me now.'

'You're dead,' said Tubbs.

Calderone looked annoyed, as if by a trifle. 'Whatsa matter with you? You *win*, man. Guess I'll just hafta take my chances in the courts.'

Tubbs was not even blinking. His eyes were brimming over with hate. Shouts from below. M-16s were being tilted up towards Calderone's back.

Calderone stared down the shotgun barrel. 'Hey,' he said, as chummy as a street wristwatch salesman. 'You ain't gonna *shoot* me, are you? That's against the law.' He dissolved into a taunting cackle of laughter. 'It's against the law!'

For Tubbs, the laughter was Calderone's last mistake. He hit him in the face with the shotgun barrel, knocking the little man against the roof edge. He rebounded and fell on his back. Tubbs stepped over him, stuck the shotgun in his face, and cocked the hammer. Calderone's laugh had been sliced off like a broken tape, and now fear lived in his coffee-brown eyes.

Tubbs' finger tightened on the trigger. '*Por mi hermano*,' he said quietly. He squeezed.

Crockett's stomach was sloshing like an off-centred washing machine and his brains were a ping-pong ball, abused by inept players. But he found that the faster he moved towards the roof, the more normal he felt. He shook off as much wooziness as he could and braced the upstairs access door, gun out.

He arrived just in time to see Tubbs strike Calderone harshly with the gun barrel. The little man fell and Tubbs was on top of him, totally unhinged, blood-red-blind with the lust for revenge.

'No!!' Crockett yelped, humping across the roof as fast as he could.

Tubbs' finger froze with the trigger half-pulled. A vibration, a breeze, the blink of an eye would send Calderone straight to hell. He seemed to not even notice Sonny behind him.

Sonny moved in now, his vision nearly normal, trying to talk Tubbs down. To shut up now would mean disaster. 'Not like this, Tubbs ... come on, partner – not like *this* ... Tubbs?'

Tubbs swallowed, eyes probing Calderone's. The drug dealer was convinced that this crazy black cop was totally off the beam. Like a cat who had been cruelly beaten, and can no longer fight or escape, Calderone lay there on his back, nearly catatonic, waiting for the end.

Five seconds was like an eon. But everyone was still there, still alive, and Calderone's eyes flickered towards Crockett for an instance. Perhaps there was a hope of redemption.

Tubbs saw it and, suddenly disgusted, snapped the trigger. The shotgun erupted fire and noise. Crockett felt the impact of the sound in his chest and flinched.

The blast singed Calderone's silver-black hair and bit a ragged gout out of the bricks behind his head. His body had jerked spastically and his eyes were clamped shut. He wet himself.

Tubbs looked to Crockett for confirmation, then dropped the shotgun at his feet, it's task apparently done.

## 13

Tubbs was pissed off, and he wasn't sure why.

He burst through the emergency room doors at Dade County General Hospital in Crockett's wake, his arm in a fresh, blindingly white sling, ignoring the protesting nurse behind him.

'Sir – ! You've lost a considerable amount of blood,' she said, matching pace, being professionally patient but firm. 'You are in no condition to be walking around just yet!'

'What the hell do you mean *transfer*?' Tubbs barked at Crockett's back. 'Transfer *where*? What's wrong with the *downtown* jail?'

Three paces ahead, a bandage hanging just out of his sight on his battered temple, Sonny explained on the run. 'Quarterback sneak, Tubbs, m'boy,' he said over his shoulder. 'We hide Calderone away in an out-of-town lockup, which buys the District Attorney – you remember Avery? – enough time to prepare a no-bail plea for the preliminary hearing tomorrow morning...'

'Detective,' the nurse butted in, meaning Crockett. 'Would you please talk some sense into this man? He's not got what you'd call a flesh wound, and he has to take this a little more serious – oh, dammit!' Her clipboard slipped through her grasp and made a masonite racket on the gleaming tile floor.

Tubbs caught up. 'Big deal, *paisan* – he still gets a

phone call, right? He'd sue everybody for a billion bucks in rights violations if he didn't get his phone call. So he gets one of his crooked judges to boogie up to the suburbs to spring him instead of downtown. The only difference I see is the longer drive.'

Crockett pasted on one of his characteristic sly grins. 'Ah, but you're missing the subtleties of working with the ultra-sophisticated Dade County Vice folks, namely, me. The catch is that nobody'll *know* Calderone is in the suburban lockup – not even Calderone himself. And by the time anyone *does* guess where we're playing hide-the-gangster, the hearing will be history and we'll have Calderone by the shorts!' He winked and added, 'We'll be transferring him in a blacked-out paddy wagon. He won't even know whether it's day or night.'

'Mr Tubbs! Get back here immediately!'

'I think your honey back there needs ya, Mister Tubbs,' said Sonny, glancing back over his shoulder as they came to swinging double doors that proclaimed EXIT to the world.

'They call me *Mister* Tubbs!' Tubbs wisecracked, also looking back.

Nurse Odetta Mason stood, arms akimbo, a comically exasperated expression on her face, fists balled, breasts thrusting aggressively against her starched white nurse's get-up, attempting to draw Tubbs back to his ward bed by sheer willpower, or maybe latent sexual charisma. Between the hem of the uniform and the clunky white work shoes lay an excellent pair of legs, in Tubbs' humble estimation. Odetta was a treat.

'She *is* a doll,' Tubbs said. 'So attentive and everything. But I wouldn't miss this thing with Calderone if I was in a wheelchair, you dig?'

'Okay,' Sonny agreed, still basking in self-glory. 'You bust anything, or start haemorrhaging or something, and I'm just gonna look the other way.'

'Such a crimefighter,' said Tubbs. He felt good despite the sickly ache in his wounded arm. They had Calderone in a jar; that's what he'd originally come down here for. Pretty soon, Rodriguez and everyone else were going to start asking him, *what's next on your agenda, MISTER Tubbs*? He was still working on the answers to that one. But meanwhile, he felt good because it had turned out that Sonny's way with Calderone seemed to be the right way.

Crockett collected his Porsche from the hotel parking lot, and Tubbs gyrated until he figured out how to open the door and climb in using only one hand.

'Shoot, man,' he griped. 'Thing like this sling could put a definite cramp in your handball form.'

'Not to mention your love life.'

'*Yours* is the one I don't wanna mention. You run all your romantic affairs like that thing with Gina? Last I saw of her she was a little stoked.'

'Gina understands,' said Crockett. 'She does what you and I do. Matter a' fact, I thought about asking her out tomorrow night after we wrap up Calderone...'

'You gonna shave?'

'Very funny.' Crockett sniffed and kept his eyes on the road, then after an uncomfortable beat, added, 'Probably not. I always forget.'

'What time is it now?'

Crockett checked. 'Nearly four a.m. Looks like the intrepid vice cops have just pulled another of their famous all-nighters... and with nary a taste of distilled spirits. Care to join me for a drink later, Tubbs, old sport?'

'Don't tell me. Elvis tends bar, too.'

'The 'gator of a thousand talents.'

The night was at its darkest, the hour or so in front of

pre-dawn. Crockett and Tubbs had the highway nearly to themselves.

The booking officer installed behind the desk at the county jail facility was named Streeter. He was a typical cell-block burnout whose unifom would fit better on a scarecrow. He had prison-grey pallor and *Night of the Living Dead* half-moons of black beneath his insomniac eyes. He looked as if he lived on caffeine, and perhaps ate human flesh every once in a while for bulk in his diet. His hair was the colour of mouldy straw, and he seemed to have a permanent dent in the side of his head from holding the telephone receiver crooked against his shoulder. He resembled, Crockett had always thought, a nerdy sixteen-year-old aritificially aged fifty years by some science-fictional torture device.

Streeter was blathering on the phone as Crockett and Tubbs approached the desk. Two uniformed cops were also waiting with reserves of patience as Streeter leisurely thumbed through a card file of that night's arrests, the 'catch of the day'.

'No, Teddy,' Streeter murmured, half-awake. 'You wanna eat with them peoples, you eat with them. I don't gotta. The Clarkes make me wanta ralph, so forget it unless you're planning on going alone –'

Crockett rapped on the desk, 'Come on, man *tonight*!' He whipped out his papers, unfolding them. 'Transfer to Orlando for prisoner Calderone.'

Streeter gave the pages a passing glance, then leaned over the file. 'Let's see... Cabanez, Cadwood... whoops, Cajun John was gone as of last night.' He removed the out-of-date card and pitched it just as an overweight jailer squeezed into the desk area.

He was lard-bellied, porcine, and smelled of cold french fries. 'All's quiet in the city zoo,' he grumbled.

'That Forbes clown mopped up the mess he made in the cell.'

'... Caldone, the guinea... Calderone. Oh yeah. Mister Bigshot.' He pulled the card.

'That's for sure,' honked the jailer. 'Stinky little squirt. How he got a city judge in here at *this* time of the morning beats the hell outta me.'

'*What*?' Tubbs' voice nearly cracked.

'Where is he – ?' demanded Crockett. 'He's not here?'

'Naw. He's gone,' said the jailer.

Sonny turned crimson. 'What do you mean *gone*? How could you let him go?!'

Streeter overrode him. 'We *had* to. The judge.'

Tubbs was across the desk grabbing a single fistful of lapel. Crockett did not stop him. 'How long ago?'

'Hands off, rye bread. You just missed him. Ten, maybe fifteen minutes ago.' He reached up to slap Tubbs' hand away but they were gone as quickly as they had appeared.

Crockett and Tubbs bolted and ran down the corridor as fast as they could manage.

Streeter was on his feet and yelling after them. 'Hey, guys, what's the big deal? Nobody skips out on two million dollars' bail!'

Crockett nearly centre-punched another uniformed street cop in his haste to get out of the building. Tubbs kept up with him all the way out into the parking lot, despite his impeding arm sling. He tried to hold his bouncing arm in place as he ran, to minimize the pain.

'Crockett!'

'No time!' Crockett yelled back. 'We've gotta move!'

If Calderone had a quarter-hour jump on them, Tubbs knew, it might as well have been a week and a half. The drug tycoon had had a contingency plan up his tailored sleeve all along... and Tubbs hoped against logic that Crockett had one too, just in case.

Crockett spun a pedestrian who decided to lag while in the crosswalk as the Porsche smoked out of the lot. He did not drop speed for a second. The brakes became irrelevant.

'That's a great way to die!' he shouted back at the crosswalker, now butt-first on the sidewalk, dazed but unharmed.

Two seconds ahead of then on Biscayne Boulevard, an intersection light blinked from yellow to red. Crockett laid on the petrol, redlining the Porsche, skimming past the front bumpers of a slew of oncoming traffic.

Tubbs' good hand had gripped the armrest, but he stayed cool.

'Call us in,' Crockett said, eyes on the road, a driving machine himself.

As they barrelled through another angrily red traffic light to the accompaniment of an equally miffed symphony of tooting and blaring car-horns, Tubbs grabbed the dashboard mike and repeated what Crockett gave him, yelling to be heard over the wind-tunnel blasts of air slicing through the open car.

Put two units at 244 Baycrest Drive right away... no, no – four *four*!'

'And the rest at the airport!' said Crockett as they rushed up on the tailgate of a station wagon poking along at forty or so.

The woman driving the station wagon made the error of glancing up into her rearview mirror. The Porsche was right on top of her and she did what most casual drivers do – she locked up like a steel door, hands frozen on the wheel, eyes front, bracing for the splintering crunch of high-speed impact.

Tubbs noted the station wagon. 'Watch out for the white lady in the –' He had begun coolly, but ended in a voice that was pitched high with sudden eye-widening terror. '*Crockett*!'

The speedometer did not budge from an even one hundred as Crockett cranked the Porsche high and wide into the breakdown lane, tearing past the station wagon on the right-hand side with inches to spare.

'Damned amateur drivers,' he muttered. 'Have a little faith, huh, Tubbs?'

As he said this, Tubbs saw the buglike 'economy car', sitting dead ahead at fifty yards, hitched up at an odd angle, emergency flashers winking yellowly away as a guy jacked the thing up to change a blown tyre.

Without a trace of crisis tension, Crockett peeled away from the shoulder and soared past the tiny automobile. The tyre-changer vaulted onto the roof in a sudden, frightened urge towards self-preservation. The swaying weight was too much for the jack and the whole mess collapsed into the road, spilling the driver. There weren't many oncoming cars to mash him flat this early in the morning.

Tubbs had felt the *ping-ping* of the wheels on his side running over the tyre iron. Not to say Sonny hadn't cut it *close*, but . . .

'Damned shame,' Crockett said, 'The way the Japanese have embarrassed us into building those little crackerbox things with the sewing machine engines.'

They blew underneath another just-red light. If they'd been five seconds faster their timing would have been perfect. This way, they were barely skinning through, and their luck could not hold.

'What airport you want the backups sent to?'

'Opa Locka. Relax, Tubbs, I see the truck. And have 'em call the tower, too.'

161

A gargantuan municipal garbage truck was making a slow, lane-consuming turn directly ahead of them. Crockett whizzed through another red light and discovered at the last second there was no room for his car between the creaking truck and the centre divider. He slid into a wheel-skidding diagonal trajectory that carried the Porsche into the oncoming lane. The two vehicles slowing down for the light panicked and screeched into a crooked V-shape as Crockett flashed through between their grilles.

'... and the others at Opa Locka,' Tubbs yelled into the radiophone. 'Call the control tower and tell then to delay if Calderone's Lear jet is scheduled for takeoff – any excuse'll do, fruit export, anything, just hold 'em on the ground for five minutes!' He listened for a beat. 'To hell with the channels, there isn't enough time!'

The light ahead did not change. It had been red all the way.

'Aw, for crying out loud ...' Crockett beefed.

'Run it, man *run* it!'

'Hang on!'

The rear wheels locked as Crockett braked, spitting grey smoke from the wheel wells as the flow of traffic through the intersection went completely beserk. More amateur drivers, bug-eyed and petrified, did nothing to get out of Crockett's way.

He stomped on the gas and straightened the shift, one-two-three. When Tubbs opened his eyes they were through the intersection and doing sixty on the Venetian Causeway.

Tubbs' eyes fixed on flashing warning lights ahead as the Porsche hit ninety. 'What's that?'

'That's a charming local attraction called the Venetian Causeway Bridge,' Sonny yelled. 'It's going up.'

162

'What're you talking about?' Tubbs shouted back as he saw the lights were mounted on the type of black-and-white striped guardrail used at railroad crossings.

'A drawbridge, Tubbs!' Sonny said with a look of peculiar exhilaration as the barrier splintered apart across the Porsche's nose. Suddenly the road seemed to go to a twenty-degree incline, then thirty.

'They only do this in movies – !' Tubbs yelled as the Porsche took to the air over the widening gap above the waterway.

The car touched down, undercarriage shrieking against the concrete ramp, sparks flying backwards in a jetwash. Sonny managed to swerve around the second guardrail.

'Only four feet of altitude, Tubbs. Hardly exciting. Hell, the gap was only ten feet wide – I jumped it once at nearly twenty-five.'

'I won't forget to put roses on your grave when you try for thirty, my man. Where the hell are we?'

'We're there, almost.'

Tubbs could see the winking safety lights of planes in flight. Each one he imagined to be Calderone, making his cockroach-like escape one more time. They had had him. They'd had him and they'd blown it. They had been outfoxed. More than ever he regretted not blowing Calderone's face into chunky soup.

They flew through the outskirts of the airport property, avoiding the parking lots. Sonny knew how to get around to the loading areas, and thence the runways, via a direct route, but of necessity it was a pathway laden with checkpoints for airport security. Two more barber-striped security gates burst into kindling around the Porsche, and in no time at all Crockett and Tubbs heard sirens behind them.

'Some security,' Crockett said. 'Look over there!'

A sleek white Lear executive jet with red markings was taxiing for takeoff. Crockett dug in his pocket for a card and handed it to Tubbs.

Tubbs looked at the 3x5 card, which read NCC11505. It was the number on the tail of the plane they were nearing. The radiophone buzzed and he picked it up, listening for an instant.

'The numbers match, Sonny! Dispatch says that Calderone was cleared for takeoff a few minutes back!'

'Tell 'em to *stop* it!'

'Too late!'

The Lear was still cantering out of its turn, nose now targetting on the narrow, blinking strip of non-commerical runway. Tubbs and Crockett heard the turbines speed up, punching several hundred decibels more of hot-wind noise rearward from the engine.

The Porsche smacked into the concrete verge of the runway doing nearly eighty miles an hour. The verge was like a speed bump, or a concrete curbing of the tyre used in parking lots, only twice as large and composed of much higher grade stone. It launched the car into the air, and this final bit of stunt flying proved far too much for the front axle.

The tail end of the plane was one hundred yards away.

Crockett's exclamation of surprise was drowned out by the hideous, grating cry of metal on pavement, as the axle snapped like a pretzel and the front end of the car took a pig's bite out of the ground. The crippled Porsche went from sixty to zero in a flat five seconds of sideways-sliding, fibreglass-chewing, tyre-eating demolition, digging twin furrows in the runway as first one wheel, then the other, exploded off the car and rolled lazily away. Augured into the ground, it sat there smoking and steaming.

Crockett was already jumping out of the cabin, gun

drawn, sprinting full speed down the runway.

Tubbs struggled to kick his way out of the Porsche. His door was sprung. He hoisted himself above the window just as the Lear jet's boom of takeoff acceleration reached him and the plane travelled forward like a bullet.

Crockett's running time was still not too shabby, but Tubbs saw the spirit go out of him all at once as he realized he did not have a hope in hell of reaching the plane, and even if he did, what did he think he was going to do? He saw Crockett run out of gas, jogging, then stopping, as his clothing flapped violently in the jet's backwash.

Then he assumed the classic pose and emptied his .45 at the departing plane with an incoherent cry of frustration.

The Lear tipped its nose skyward and curved up into the air gracefully, a perfect takeoff. It banked in the night sky and then headed off towards the Carribean.

Tubbs finally extricated himself from the automobile, and walked slowly towards Crockett, who stayed where he was, gazing into space, the automatic slack in his hand, pointed earthward.

The two detectives watched the receding lights of the jet diminish, until they could no longer be seen. Crockett and Tubbs seemed quite tiny, standing alone in the centre of the vast and desolate plain of concrete.

'I'm sorry, Tubbs, I –' His voice lost the words. 'I'm sorry.'

Tubbs was still looking into the sky. The jet had long since vanished into a hazy marine layer of clouds.

'It's not your fault, man.'

Car doors slammed, and soon guns were pointed and arch-tough orders were being shouted at them by the minions of airport security.

'Real buncha all-stars,' Sonny said. 'Put your hands up, Tubbs, till we can tell these bozos who we are.'

## 14

They made the ride back to the Dade County Metro Station in the back of a squad car, behind a felon-proof steel mesh screen, in that part of the cruiser featuring no inside door handles for the convenience of the passengers.

'Two million bucks,' Crockett shook his head. 'Calderone grosses so much cash he can drop two million bucks, just like that, to avoid spending a night in jail. Two million to foil my neat little strategy . . . didn't know I was worth that much.'

'Maybe they can use some of it to repair our . . . uh, damage estimates,' Tubbs said. 'Y'know – two cars totalled, angry citizens billing the city for their bent fenders, repairs to the gates at the bridge and airport, patching up the runway . . . you sure like to do things in style, Sonny.' He shifted in his seat, favouring his cast. 'Not to mention our personal damages . . . You know. this plaster thing really kind of *hurts*.'

'Rodriguez is probably hitting the ceiling by now,' Sonny observed. He knew both of them were avoiding talking about what was really on their minds, filling up the dead air with this sort of chit-chat. After one uncomfortable silence too many, he said, 'He'll be back, Tubbs. New name, new people, new contacts . . . but he'll be back. Hell, this is the Sunshine State, right? He won't be able to resist. More snow comes through here than the Swiss Alps.'

Tubbs nodded grimly.

'I'm gonna be filling out reports for a *week*,' Sonny lamented.

'Get Elvis to take shorthand.'

He ignored it, probing. 'Uh... I guess you've got a job to get back to up north, right?'

Tubbs emitted a morose little laugh, then looked at Crockett strangely. 'You kidding? Use that computer mind of yours to replay the past couple of days, man – after the performance I put on down here hits the fans, I'll be lucky to claw my humble way back onto the payroll as a meter maid.'

Crockett sighed again. Tubbs was coming to recognize the sigh as another of Crockett's repertoire of gestures, like the way he was constantly interrupting people. It was a kind of deep draw of breath, sucked in luxuriously, voluminously, like rich tobacco, then expelled in an express train rush through both nostrils, with the eyes set and the brow slightly furrowed, as if annoyed at a trifle. 'I think you and I could use a little attitude alteration. You still have that Camaro parked at the station?'

'Yeah, *mon*. My bill would fry your eyes.'

'You up for a little drive from there?'

'What do you have in mind?'

'A great little dockside beer joint down in the Keys, called Stanley's Wharf. Terrific for people with mood problems, who are averse to city bars.'

Tubbs glanced at his Teddy Prentiss dealer's watch. 'You know a bar that's open at... hey, this damned thing has stopped!' He tapped it, like an irate customer in a silent movie comedy.

Crockett laughed aloud at Tubbs' predicament. 'I'll give it to Elvis. Midnight snack.'

'I know it's nowhere near midnight.'

'Try 5.45 in the morning,' Crockett said, consulting his own wristwatch.

'So, you know a bar that's open at six a.m. on a Sunday morning?'

Crockett gave him an utterly jaded look. 'Does Leslie Gore cry at her parties?'

'I take that to mean *yes*, in Florida-speak.' He yawned and snapped to. 'You got it. I have no desire to be out of doors when the sun comes up, man, not after this night and not in my current state of mind.'

'Stanley's is just the place. Inside, it's timeless. The dark in there *never* changes.'

'*And* I got nothing better booked in at the moment,' Tubbs put in.

'And after you knock back a few shots,' Crockett said, 'I might get around to asking you if you've ever considered a fulfilling career in Southern law enforcement.'

'Yeah, I'm kinda stuck in a dead-end job right now,' Tubbs smiled. 'I need a little . . . excitement in my life.'

'I take it that's New York-speak for *yes*?'

'Maybe,' he said. 'Maybe.'


Crockett drove the Camaro. He and Tubbs made it to Stanley's Wharf just as the sun began to peer pinkly over the eastern horizon, signifying the beginning of a new day for all the rest of the local folk.